# BLACK BART'S TREASURE

Phil Carradice

D0807430

Pont

To Bob, Anne, John and Catherine,
remembering our walk along
the beach at Kiawah Island,
where Johnny Four Toes was born.

Published in 2007 by Pont Books, an imprint of
Gomer Press, Llandysul, Ceredigion, SA44 4JL

ISBN 978 1 84323 740 2

A CIP record for this title is available from the British Library.

This book is published with the financial support of the
Welsh Books Council.

Printed and bound in Wales at
Gomer Press, Llandysul, Ceredigion

## Chapter One

# The Treasure Map

'When they 'angs you,' said old Jethro, 'your face turns black, black as a pirate's flag, and your eyes pops out so that you looks like one of them toads you find in lily ponds. Your tongue grows huge and sticks out six inches from your mouth. Like an adder, it is, coming out of its 'ole in the ground.'

Jethro's head shot suddenly forward. His blackened tongue snaked across the stumps of his few remaining teeth and he leered at his listeners. Harriet Amos felt her stomach turn as fear gathered like a thunderstorm in her belly.

'That's what happens to pirates when they catches 'em,' said Jethro.

The children stared, spellbound, at the old man. For thirty seconds there was total silence as Jethro glared at each of them in turn, enjoying the moment.

'Get on with you,' said Ben, at last. 'You ain't ever seen any pirates.'

Harriet glared at the boy, angry that the mood had been broken. It wasn't often that Jethro, the old peddler who wandered the villages of south Pembrokeshire, stopped to talk to anybody, let alone a group of youngsters nobody considered much use for anything. Ben was always the restless one. No story was ever likely to hold him for long, no matter what it was. He preferred climbing on the cliffs at Freshwater East or St Govan's to listening to tales of adventure and piracy from people like Jethro.

'Really?' said the old man, fixing Ben with a cold stare. 'Oh, I seen 'em all right, don't you worry about that. I've seen Black Bart's men, or what there was left of 'em, hanging there on Execution Dock, jerking and dancing on the ends of their ropes. Oh, I seen 'em all right, believe me.'

He paused and looked around, furtively. 'All the ringleaders, all except for one. And him I hopes never to see again.'

Ben snorted. 'Jethro, the only pirates you ever saw were the thieving crows on Squire Campbell's fields.'

There was a low rumble of laughter from the other boys and Ben pushed himself to his feet. He stood at the top of the bank, tall and arrogant, and gazed down the field towards the cliff top. A faint silver glimmer showed where the land dropped away into the sea.

'Stupid stories,' he snorted. 'Save them for the girls. I'm going bird-nesting – anyone coming with me? Harriet?'

He looked over meaningfully at her, then he took off down the slope, the other boys straggling reluctantly behind him. Old Jethro stared after them, then shrugged and began to pack up his gear.

'No, Jethro,' Harriet whispered, 'don't go. Tell me more, please? Tell me about Black Bart and his crew.'

Jethro glanced up at her. 'Another time, girl, another time.'

He shouldered his battered canvas bag and slouched

6

away up the lane towards the village. Harriet watched him go, cursing Ben for his impatience. The old man hadn't said much but every word he'd uttered had enthralled her. The thought of Black Bart, the pirate chief, his galleons and his treasure, filled her head so that she could hardly think of anything else.

'Harriet?'

Harriet felt a hand on her arm and when she looked down saw that Mary, small, blonde and a year or two younger, was pulling at her sleeve.

'Come on, Harriet, he's gone. Let's go and look at my new kittens.'

Harriet nodded, half-heartedly, and allowed herself to be led across the field towards Mary's back garden. Kittens didn't interest her but she would like to learn more about Black Bart, and Jethro was clearly the man to tell her.

That night Harriet sat in the dark, low-roofed cottage where she lived with her mother and father. All evening she slumped in front of the fire and tried to conjure shapes out of the flames. She tried to imagine Black Bart, the pirate, but she had no idea what he even looked like. Every time she tried to picture a face in the ash or on the bark of a burning branch, it seemed only to turn into the shape and image of old Jethro.

It was late and the fire was beginning to die when she suddenly asked, 'What was Black Bart like?'

Her father sat back on the settle where he was idly working at the fire. He put down his stick and glanced at her. 'Black Bart Roberts?' he said. 'The pirate? He came from north of the river, a place called Little Newcastle, I think. Close to Fishguard, it is. *Barti Ddu*, that's what they call him up there, on account of how they speak Welsh. Why do you want to know, girl?'

Harriet explained how Jethro had stopped to talk to them that afternoon.

'Don't you go listening to old Jethro's tales,' her father snorted, the faintest hint of amusement in his voice. 'I shouldn't think he ever came within fifty miles of Black Bart.' He picked up his twig and began to poke it at the fire once more. 'Black Bart died, oh, I don't know, maybe twenty or even thirty years ago, killed on board his ship somewhere off the coast of Africa. He was hunted down by the navy, I think, all his crew killed along with him or put on trial and hung for piracy.'

'But what did he look like?' Harriet insisted. 'Do you know?'

Her father shrugged. 'Can't say as I ever saw him. I was only a boy at the time and he didn't sail much around these parts. There's been plenty of other pirates round here, mind. John Callice, for a start, he used to have his base over in Angle, at an inn called the Point House – a real hot bed for pirates that was. And Howell Davis, he came from Milford. But Black Bart? No, he sailed out in the Indies and Africa, not round here.'

He paused, shaking his head. Harriet was not sure if he was regretting the fact or was glad that Black Bart had stayed well away from his native country. 'They say he used to wear a red coat and a waistcoat – a bit of a gentleman, like. At least, that's how he fancied himself. He didn't allow any drinking on his ship, unusual for a pirate.'

John Amos sat upright and leaned his shoulders back against the wall. He was lucky: his farm had good fields and Squire Campbell was always calling on him to talk about crop rotation and things that Harriet didn't understand. But it was still hard work, out there all day in all weathers. And a late night talk about pirates with a daughter whose strange interests and imagination he could hardly begin understand was something he really did not need just now.

'That's enough silly stories for tonight,' he muttered. 'Don't you go filling your head with any nonsense old Jethro might tell you. Black Bart's dead: he isn't going to be bothering you and that's all there is to it. Now, we've got an early start in the morning if we want to get to market before anyone else, so up the stairs with you, quick.'

Harriet climbed the dark staircase to the low-roofed attic that was her bedroom. It was hot and stuffy in there, the heat from the fire below seeming to seep up through the cracks in the floorboards. She threw open the heavy casement and leaned against the ledge. She stared out into the night, feeling a slight breeze on her face and neck.

There was so much she wanted to know, about Black Bart and the pirates and about the world out there, beyond the village – beyond the county of Pembrokeshire. There was so much to learn, so much to see and do. One day, she told herself, she would escape the confines of Stackpole village; one day she would see the world.

The sudden bark of a fox, close up in the spinney across the green, made her jump in fright. She slammed the casement shut and dived for her bed. With the rough blanket pulled high over her head, she was asleep in minutes.

Harriet and her father were awake early the next morning and by six they were already on the road to Pembroke town. The day was fine but this early in the morning the air was cool and they covered the miles easily. Once, John Amos stopped, gazing eagerly around, a puzzled frown on his face.

'What is it, Father?'

The burly farmer shrugged and stood in the road, listening intently. All was quiet and, presently, he walked on, wheeling the handcart that carried their vegetables and produce.

'I'm not sure. I just fancied that I heard something in the field. But there's nothing there. Come on, keep up.'

Harriet glanced nervously towards the hedge that ran along the side of the road. It was wise to be careful – you never knew who might be watching. The hedge was thick and high and she could not see beyond it. She listened but heard nothing, not even birds chirping. She shook her head and ran quickly after her father.

When they arrived in Pembroke, they set up their stall close to the town's Golden Cross. Already there were dozens of people about, many of them servants from the big houses further up Main Street, and the town's narrow thoroughfares were thronged with the early risers.

'Should be a good day,' said Harriet's father to the woman on the stall alongside him. 'There seem to be a lot of strangers about.'

The woman nodded. 'Two schooners came in late last night and moored at the quay beneath the castle. They'll be after fresh food, I shouldn't wonder, after spending all those days at sea.'

The woman was right. By noon they had sold everything. The pieces of crochet work that Harriet and her mother had made during the long winter nights had been snapped up by eager shoppers. Harriet even managed to sell the few potatoes that her father let her grow in a patch of ground alongside the back wall of their cottage. She felt the warm glow of the two shilling pieces in her palm and knew that, together with the other pennies and farthings hidden in her shoe – coins she had earned from other sales over the weeks – she now had ten whole shillings to her name. It was a good sum, she thought, a fine return for all her hard work.

'That's it for today,' said her father, wiping his hands on the legs of his breeches. 'We've done well. You head off home, girl. I'm for a quart of ale in the King's Arms. Tell your mother I'll be back presently.'

Harriet slipped easily away, knowing they would not see her father much before midnight. She hoped he would not spend too much of their hard-earned wages.

The afternoon was hot, the wind of early morning having now dropped away, and Harriet felt sticky and uncomfortable as she strode along the road, trying to keep in the shade of the tall hedges. Even when she got near the coast, the air was still oppressive and she was grateful when she finally came to the thick woodlands outside the village. She flung herself down alongside a small brook that ran down the hill and, with a sigh of relief, dipped her hands into the water. Eagerly she splashed her face and arms. She bent over the stream to drink and at that moment saw the reflection in the water.

11

'God preserve me!' she screamed, leaping to her feet and backing away in alarm.

'Don't shout, girl,' said old Jethro. 'It's only me. I won't hurt you.'

Relief flooded through her body as she recognised the peddler. Even in her fear she wondered quite how the man managed to move about so quietly – like a cat, Harriet thought. 'Jethro,' she said, 'you frightened the wits out of me.'

When she looked at him, however, Harriet began to wonder who had been most frightened. Jethro's face was curiously pale: his normal brown tan seemed to have disappeared. The old man's hands shook as he eased the canvas bag off his shoulder and sat down beside the stream.

'Are you all right, Jethro?' Harriet asked. 'You look strange.'

'Had a bit of a fright, girl, that's all. I just saw . . .'

He stopped and shuddered.

'Saw what?' asked Harriet.

Jethro shook his head. He took off his hat and ran his old gnarled fingers through the thin strands of his hair. 'Not what, girl, who.' He lapsed into silence.

Harriet waited.

'Someone I'd hoped never to see again,' Jethro whispered eventually. 'Fair scared me half to death, I must say.'

Harriet sat down beside him, eased off her shoes and let her feet lie, luxuriously, in the cool water of the brook. She gazed up at old Jethro and grinned. 'I thought pirates didn't get frightened,' she said.

Jethro laughed, the sound hollow and echoing in the

stillness of the wood. 'This one does. Besides, I ain't been a pirate for years. Not since they killed Black Bart Roberts.'

'Did you know him, Jethro? Did you know Black Bart? Did you ever sail with him? Tell me, I want to know.'

The thirst for knowledge was strong and Harriet knew that this was her chance to find out more about the pirates who so fascinated her. Here, at the edge of the stream, in the quietness of the hot August afternoon, there was no-one like Ben to spoil the telling of the story. Jethro, however, seemed a little reluctant to start. He stared into the gloom of the woods, as if he was trying to pick out some strange or dangerous figure that might be lurking there. At last, he seemed to pull himself together and turned towards her.

'Aye, girl, I knew him. I was with him almost till the end. A short life and a merry one, that's what he said he wanted. And that's what he got, all right. Betrayed, he was, betrayed and then cut to pieces by grapeshot. Know what that is, girl?'

Harriet shook her head.

'Grapeshot is what they fires from cannons on board ship. But it's not like a cannon ball; it just scatters when you fires it. Thousands of little balls an' bits of lead all flying about the place. Cuts you to bits, it does. An' it caught old Bart in the throat, just as the battle started. Dead in a second, he were, the greatest pirate that ever lived, cut down just like that.'

He snapped his fingers, the sound suddenly loud and startling in the quiet of the clearing.

'Four hundred ships we took in just three years on

the account, him in his blood-red coat and that damned great feather in his cap. Grand, he looked, standing there on the quarter deck and everyone running round at his orders. Until he were betrayed. Otherwise they'd never have caught him. It were one of his own men what turned him in, girl, one of his own sort.'

He paused and leaned closer. 'Beware a man who limps, girl, beware a sailor with four toes on his right foot.' Jethro pointed, deliberately, at his own leg.

Harriet gazed at him, fascinated but appalled. 'Four toes?'

'Aye, girl, one toe missing and the others all crumpled up and crabbing sideways like a badly reefed lugger in a storm. Makes him limp but don't let that fool you. Fast as lightning when he wants to be is Johnny Four Toes. Worser than the Devil he is. Remember, four toes – and a gold tooth up 'ere.'

He wrenched open his mouth and stabbed with his finger at a spot on his upper jaw.

Harriet shivered with fear. 'Did Johnny Four Toes betray Black Bart?'

Jethro nodded. 'That he did. John Jessup, that's his real name. He'd been with Bart since the beginning but he took to drink, he did. Now, they says Black Bart didn't 'ave no drinking on his ship. Not true, girl, not true. He couldn't stop 'em drinking, hard as he tried. He only drank tea, himself, and he did his best to keep them sailors off the grog. But it weren't no good.'

'What's grog?' asked Harriet, her eyes wide with wonder.

'Rum, girl, rum. It's what every sailor wants when he retires, when he comes off the account.'

14

Harriet stared at him, not understanding.

Jethro shook his head and breathed out in exasperation. 'Don't you know nothing? *Going on the account*, that's what they calls it when you takes up with pirates, when you becomes a buccaneer. Anyway Johnny Four Toes, 'e was a drunkard – a good gunner, mind, could shoot the spots out of a playing card at fifty paces. And he was educated, second only to Bart himself in those terms. But drunk most of the time, 'e was. And Bart didn't like that.'

He lay back against the bank and closed his eyes. The colour had returned to his cheeks, Harriet noticed, and he seemed more like the Jethro of old. It was as if the talking had calmed his nerves.

'Interested in pirates, are you?' Jethro said suddenly.

Harriet nodded. 'Yes. I want to go to sea. I want to search for treasure, pirate treasure.'

Jethro said nothing, just lay there, breathing deeply and easily. He seemed to be considering Harriet's words. Finally, his eyes jerked open, his stare boring into her. Harriet had never realised before just how blue and clear the old man's eyes really were. 'Then you'll be needing a map, won't you, a map that shows you where the treasure's hidden?'

A thrill of excitement shot into Harriet's belly. She leaned in close to the old peddler. 'Have you got one? Have you got a pirate's map?'

Jethro glanced around, scanning the woods for any hidden watchers, and then reached into his bag. Carefully he pulled out a small oilskin packet. He held it up in front of Harriet's eyes and nodded. 'Oh, aye, I've got one. This 'ere map is the key to Black Bart's treasure. An' what a treasure that is. It ain't ever been found though there's hundreds as have been looking for it over the years. People thinks as he buried it all on Los Idols off Sierra Leone. But he didn't. Oh, no, he kept his gold a lot closer to home – a lot, lot closer.'

Jethro began to laugh. He laughed until the tears ran down his cheeks, leaving long streaks in the dirt and grime that coated his face. Finally, he seemed to pull himself together and began to wave the packet in front of Harriet's eyes. She reached out to take it but the old peddler snatched it away and held it tightly to his chest.

'It'll cost you, girl. Nobody gets nothing for nothing in this 'ere world. How much have you got?'

Harriet knew she had to have the map. She glanced towards her shoes, still sitting on the bank over the brook – and the money that was carefully hidden in them. So much hard work had gone into earning that money but, despite all the warnings sounding inside her head, she knew that the map spelled adventure and, who knew, maybe even fortune. 'I've got ten shillings,' she said eagerly.

The peddler coughed and began to grin. Then he seemed to catch himself and he stared at Harriet through narrowed eyes. 'Ten shillings?' he hissed. 'It's worth thirty times more, a hundred times. But I reckons as I'm on a lee shore. Needs must, I suppose, and I needs to get away for a bit, see, girl? And ten shillings is better than nothing, I reckons. So, 'ere, take it, it's yours.'

Harriet felt the oilskin packet in her fingers. It was thin and smooth but she felt sure that it contained the whole world. She passed across the money and, with the packet in one hand and her shoes in the other, stood up to go.

'Beware the limping man, girl,' said Jethro. 'Beware Johnny Four Toes. He'll be after Black Bart's treasure, just like you. When he comes for you, it'll be in the night and then you'd best run for your life.'

Harriet felt his grip, hard and angry, on her arm and knew that he spoke the truth. And suddenly she knew why Jethro was so frightened.

They stared into each other's eyes and the old man smiled for the last time and nodded. 'That's right, girl; I've seen him; Johnny's back.'

The crash of a pheasant in the undergrowth made Harriet spin around in alarm. When she turned back, Jethro had gone, as suddenly as he had appeared. Harriet felt panic claw at her chest. Maybe it hadn't been a pheasant! She turned around, slowly and carefully, and stared, wondering if Johnny Four Toes was watching. She shook her head, dismissing the idea as stupid. Even if he existed, Johnny would be more interested in Jethro than in her. He'd never know she had the map.

She pushed the packet under the waistband of her skirt and set off up the hill towards the village.

*Chapter Two*

# Johnny Four Toes

Harriet strode briskly across the village green. She kept her head bent low, and her dark hair swung backwards and forwards across her cheek like the loose sail of a schooner. The far hedge was the harbour wall, she reckoned, and if she could just get there before the squall hit . . .

She pushed the notion aside and laughed at herself. Forget fantasy, she told herself, feeling the soft bulk of the oilskin packet against her stomach: this is real adventure. She reached the shadow of the yew hedge where it was cool and sat down with her back against one of the bigger tree stumps.

'Now, then,' she said to herself, 'let me see what I've got.' Carefully, she untied the strings around the package and unfolded the outer covering. Inside lay a single sheet of parchment, folded into two. Harriet smoothed the paper across her knee, feeling it crinkle like an autumn leaf over her skirt. Her heart beat faster as the crude drawing of an island seemed to leap off the page.

The island was shaped like a figure eight, narrow in the middle with two small hills at each end. The valley between the hills was flanked by cliffs on one side and a small sandy beach on the other. The whole island could be barely more than half a mile in length. The map showed little enough to help any sailor to locate the island. Harriet shrugged. It hardly mattered; she would not have understood anyway. As far as she was concerned, it could have been anywhere. All that mattered was that she now owned the map.

She stared at the parchment, glad she'd bothered to attend the Circulating School that came to the village each winter. Squire Campbell had supported the clergyman who came one day and suggested that the village children might like to learn to read during the quiet winter months. Unlike Ben and the other boys, Harriet had been happy to go along each morning, sitting for hours in one of the Squire's barns, learning her letters and working her way through the Bible, the only reading material they had. There had been times when she wondered why she bothered – now she knew!

Turning the map over, Harriet saw, on the back, some straggling and badly written lines. She squinted at them for some time. It seemed to be a poem.

'Where does it lie? Ten paces from the mouth.
Which way does it face? It looks due south.
What's buried there? Doubloons and silver, gold.
Who put it there? Why *Barti Ddu* so bold.
It lies due north of lonely Flat Holm Isle,
Such gold will make the House of Lords to smile.'

What on earth did all that mean, Harriet wondered? It made no sense. What was buried – and where? *Barti Ddu* was obvious – her father had said that was what they called Black Bart in the north of the county, where the people all spoke Welsh. But what on earth was the House of Lords? And where was Flat Holm Isle? It was all so exciting but infuriating, too. She clenched her fists in temper.

Suddenly, a dark shadow fell across the map and Harriet glanced up in alarm.

'What's this, then?' Ben was standing above her, arms folded across his chest and his foot tapping. What chance would she have to work things out for herself if he caught even the whiff of adventure?

'Well?' he demanded, staring down at the parchment resting across Harriet's knee.

Hurriedly, Harriet folded the map and put it back into its oilskin packet. 'Nothing to concern you, Ben Walters,' she said, retying the strings and pushing the packet into her waistband.

Ben glared at her, unsure whether to challenge. He was not used to Harriet being so bold. 'I'm going down to Barafundle Beach,' he said at last. 'Want to come?'

Harriet shook her head and stood up. 'I've got to get home. Mother needs my help.'

'Suit yourself.'

They glared at each other before Harriet turned on her heel and strode away. When, a minute later, she paused at the door to her cottage and glanced back over her shoulder, the boy was still standing in front of the hedge, staring after her. Let him look, Harriet thought; he doesn't know anything. I've got the map, that's all that counts.

She slipped into the cottage, noticing that her mother was out on the long patch of grass at the back of the house. She was collecting washing off the hedges where, earlier in the day, she had carefully laid it to dry.

Quickly, Harriet ran up the stairs to her room and crossed the creaking floorboards to the wall beside the casement. Alongside the casement frame the wattle and daub had cracked and, working carefully, she eased back the plaster. It was a perfect hiding place, somewhere to keep secrets, away from prying eyes. The oilskin packet fitted easily into the gap.

'Be safe,' she whispered, replaced the plaster and went back to the staircase.

She would tell her parents about the map tomorrow, she decided. Tonight, with Father back late from Pembroke, his belly full of good Welsh ale, would be the wrong time. He would be angry that she had given Jethro money, even though he would probably have spent just as much on beer in the King's Arms. He wouldn't understand her fascination with Black Bart and the pirates. He would call Jethro's map a fake and probably end up by throwing it into the fire. No, she decided, this needed careful handling and tonight was not the time to tell her parents what she had done.

When Harriet reached the ground floor once more, her mother was coming in through the door, her arms full of clean washing. 'Back already?' she asked. 'Where's your father?'

Harriet told her about their day, taking care to miss out her encounter with old Jethro. Her mother shook her head when she heard about the King's Arms but said nothing. Together, they began to lay the table for supper, Harriet's mind full of the wonderful map. When she found Black Bart's treasure, she thought, there would be no more of this. Then her mother would have servants to work for her – there would be no more laying tables and collecting washing. She would live like the Squire's wife.

But how could she find out where the island was located? There was nothing on the parchment to give the slightest clue, at least not to a landlubber like her. She liked that term, 'landlubber', although she couldn't remember where she had heard it. Maybe it was something Ben had said? Thinking of Ben made her wonder if she should enlist his help. He always seemed so sure of himself, so full of adventure and ideas. Maybe she would ask him to help in the search for the treasure? The trouble was, whenever they were together, working in the fields or just sitting and gossiping on the village green, they always seemed to end up arguing. Ben liked to be in control but this was her map, her adventure. There was so much to think about, so much to consider.

'Come on, Harriet,' her mother called, startling her out of her trance. 'Wake up! Put the skillet on the fire. Supper won't make itself, you know.'

Harriet slept badly that night, her dreams full of pirates in scarlet coats standing on the decks of magnificent men-of-war. There were sun-tanned sailors on the deck and one of them walked with a limp. Once she woke, scared and sweating, sitting bolt upright in her bed, sure that someone or something was scratching on the outside of the casement. It was too dark to see and she had no taper or flint to light her stub of candle. She sat there, holding her breath, watching and waiting, but there was no further sound and after a while she lay down and drifted back to sleep.

The following day Harriet was back at work in her father's fields. Most of the children from the village were there, picking stones out of the earth before the field could be ploughed and sowed next spring. It was a back-breaking task and Harriet had little time to think about Black Bart's map.

'This is too much like hard work,' complained Ben as they finally stopped for food. 'I prefer hay making. At least then you get the chance of a few rabbits. All we'll get today is an ache between the shoulder blades.'

Before she could stop herself, Harriet turned on him with a smile. 'That's typical of you, Ben Walters, always thinking about your stomach. It'll do you good to do a bit of hard work for a change.'

He threw himself down and propped his back against the wheel of a cart. He rummaged in one of the large wicker baskets that had been brought from the village and pulled out a cold potato. Grinning good-naturedly at Harriet, he bit into it and chewed contentedly. Several of the boys from the village joined him but Harriet walked over to sit with the girls and knelt down alongside her friend Mary, helping her to make daisy chains.

When next she looked up, she saw Ben and two boys wandering away towards the hedge that lined the adjacent field. 'Where are they going?' she asked.

'Ben said something about a pheasant's nest,' said Mary. 'It's over there in the next field. They've just gone to find it.'

Harriet lay back and closed her eyes. She was tired. The sun on her face was warm and, after the restlessness of the previous night, sleep came easily. She did not dream but went immediately into a deep and dark unconsciousness. How long she lay there she did not know but she was jolted suddenly awake by the sound of a piercing scream. She struggled to her feet, eyes still blurred and unfocussed. People were shouting and seemed to be running everywhere.

'What is it?' Harriet demanded. 'What's going on?'

'It's a body!' Mary shouted. 'Ben's found a body.'

A cold hand seemed to clutch at Harriet's chest. A body? Almost before she knew it, she found herself sprinting towards the far field. Ahead of her she could see men and boys clustered near the hedgerow. Even as she ran, she knew what she would find.

'Harriet, come back,' she heard Mary call from far behind.

A man from the village was suddenly in front of her, barring the way with outstretched arms. 'Stay back,' he ordered but she dodged his flailing arms and ran on.

Panting and afraid, she came at last to the fringe of the group. She could see her father, his face pale with shock. And Ben was there, too, standing self-importantly alongside the body, but when his eyes met hers, he held up his hand to stop her coming closer. Almost imperceptibly, he shook his head. Harriet opened her mouth to speak, but the words would not come out.

'Who is it?' asked the man in front of her.

Harriet did not wait for the answer. She knew who it would be and pushed her way to the front of the crowd. Old Jethro was lying on his back at the foot of the hedge, his throat slit neatly from ear to ear. The blood on his neck had dried to a dark brown stain, as dark as the tan on his weather-beaten arms but his face, Harriet noticed, was strangely white, as if all the blood had been drained out. His blue eyes stared sightlessly upwards. Of his battered canvas bag there was no sign.

'Oh, Jethro,' she breathed, 'I thought you were going to get away.'

Her father stared at her, his eyes wide and questioning. He opened his mouth to speak but Harriet knew she didn't need to be interrogated just now. She spun on her heel and walked purposefully away.

That night, when her father came home, it was with the news that Squire Campbell had taken charge of the affair. 'Not that it'll go anywhere,' sighed John Amos. 'Anybody could have killed him. The Squire will be wasting his time.'

'Why's that?' asked his wife. 'The Squire is an honest man; he'll do his best to find the murderer.'

John shrugged. 'Oh, I know he will but there's no witness, no weapon. All he's got is a body. Nobody round here had a quarrel with Jethro, not that we know of anyway. If you ask me it was probably one of those tinkers who were camped here last year. He had some sort of argument with them at the time, I seem to remember. I don't know of anyone else who might have done it. But then, those tinkers have been gone over twelve months.'

He stopped and looked at Harriet. 'Do you know anything about this, girl? You've been pretty close to old Jethro lately, what with your tales of pirates and suchlike.'

Harriet shook her head but did not trust herself to speak. Her father stared at her intently and Harriet could not hold his gaze. She dropped her eyes and pretended to be picking at a seam of her dress. She heard her father speaking but knew she did not dare to look at him.

'I just thought you were about to say something

earlier today when we found the body. You really don't know anything?' Again Harriet shook her head.

Her father sighed. 'Well, it's in the Squire's hands now. Poor old Jethro, I wonder who could have done something like that to him. I wouldn't have thought the man had an enemy in the world.'

*If only you knew*, Harriet said bitterly to herself. There were so many people who might want the old peddler dead, people from his past – and one in particular. She knew it was Johnny Four Toes. It had to be; Jethro had said he'd seen him in the village. And if the pirate was looking for Black Bart's map, then she might be the next on his list. What if the old man talked before Johnny killed him?

Harriet knew she should tell her father or the Squire about Johnny Four Toes, about the man she believed had killed old Jethro, but the thought of the treasure map hidden upstairs in her room was stronger than the fear. She was not going to lose the chance for adventure and riches, no matter what Johnny Four Toes might do to her. For the moment she would keep her knowledge to herself, she decided – and the map!

When she climbed the stairs with her candle an hour later, Harriet went, first, to the casement and made sure it was firmly bolted. Then she checked her hiding place. The map was still there, sitting snugly in the gap behind the plaster. She climbed into bed and lay there, thinking desperately about what she should do. When sleep finally overcame her, she had still not decided.

When she awoke, she knew immediately that something was wrong. It was obviously late into the night because the fire in the room below had died and its

26

comforting glow had long since disappeared. And yet her bedroom was bathed in light. The casement was open and the light of the full moon was shining brightly into the room. It shone onto the floor and onto the foot of her bed. And it shone onto the blade of the wicked-looking knife that the man at her bedside was holding.

'Who are you?' Harriet gasped, trying to ease herself into a sitting position. 'What are you doing here?'

The man reached out and in one quick, decisive movement pushed her back onto the bed. Harriet gasped as the knife wavered in the air, a few inches from her throat. The man's hand was on her chest and she could feel the raw power of his body. 'Stay still, girl.'

The voice was hoarse and low and the sense of menace was so strong that Harriet felt she could have reached out and grabbed it. The man was dressed in a leather coat that reached down almost to the floor but Harriet could still see heavy boots, sailors' boots. A silver earring flashed in the man's left ear.

'Do you know who I am?' he whispered.

Harriet shook her head, trying to quell rising waves of panic and sickness.

The man laughed, soundlessly, his head thrown back and mouth wide open. A gold tooth glinted and, despite herself, Harriet glanced quickly down at his feet.

The man followed the direction of her gaze, raised one booted foot into the air and smiled. 'That's right, my dear, I can see you've heard of me. Johnny Four Toes at your service.'

*Chapter Three*

# Hunted

It felt like hours though later Harriet realised that it had only been a matter of minutes. She lay there, trying to keep her breathing low and regular. What had happened to her mother and father? Had Johnny killed them or were they still alive downstairs? What was going to happen to her? Her mind was spinning.

All the while Johnny Four Toes sat quietly alongside her, waiting, staring silently, almost gently, at her face. 'Well, girl,' he whispered at last, 'have you got it?'

Harriet shook her head. 'I don't know what you mean.'

Johnny sighed and made a careful pretence of studying the fingertips of his left hand. The other hand, the one that held the knife, rested easily on Harriet's shoulder. She could feel the sharp point of the blade as it pricked into the skin of her neck.

'Of course you do. Black Bart's map. Don't deny it. Old Jethro told me he'd sold it to you before – before, well, shall we say before he sailed off into a new sort of anchorage.'

He laughed, low, quietly and with menace. Harriet suddenly realised that her parents were still safe – why else would Johnny Four Toes be making such an effort to keep quiet? They slept downstairs in a room alongside the main door so Johnny must have got in through her casement window.

'Why did you kill Jethro?' she said.

The pirate turned his face towards her and smiled. There was no warmth in the expression. 'He was going to warn you. I saw it in his eyes. Oh, he said he wouldn't blab, wouldn't say a word, but I knew the minute I let him go, he'd have been on his way here, ready to tell you all about me. And you, of course, would have popped along to see your precious Squire. And that would have been it, game up. So I'm afraid old Jethro had to go.'

From far away came the sound of a church clock striking. Harriet counted the strokes – one, two, three o'clock. It would start to get light in another hour or so. Could she keep him talking that long? As if sensing her thoughts, Johnny leaned forward and glared into her eyes.

'Enough talking, I want my map. Where is it?'

'It's not your map,' Harriet hissed. 'It's Black Bart's.'

Johnny snorted and his eyes blazed. 'Black Bart? He's been dead these twenty years. Twenty years and most of that time I've spent sweating and breaking my back in the Cape Coast mines. That's where they sent all Bart's men, out to the mines – leastways the ones they didn't hang. Working in those mines was like a damned death sentence in itself. And do you know what kept me going all those years? The thought of the treasure. Don't I deserve it? I was with him right from the beginning, girl, so if anybody deserves to get his hands on that treasure, it's me.'

Harriet glared up at the man and, despite the fear washing and swirling like seawater in her belly, knew that she had to speak. 'You betrayed him. You turned him in. You deserve nothing.'

Her words obviously hit the mark because Johnny's

face suddenly seemed to darken. A small nerve began to twitch in his cheek and Harriet sensed that it would not take much to push this murderous man over the edge of reason.

'So what?' said Johnny Four Toes. 'We were pirates, not parsons. Live by the sword, die by the sword, that was the rule. Bart knew that. And what reward did I get. Did they give me a pardon? Not on your life. A quick trial at Cape Corso and then they sent me to the mines to work like a slave. And there I waited. Oh yes, I waited, girl, waited while the others all died like flies around me. I waited, knowing that the treasure was out there. I just had to find it.'

He stood up, his body outlined against the light from the open window. Even in her fear Harriet could see that he was not tall but the muscles and taut sinews of his arms showed the immense power of the man. He seemed inclined to talk and Harriet knew she was not about to stop him.

'Not long before he died Bart slipped away from the squadron, him and a handful of his most trusted men. He was gone six, maybe eight weeks. We were lying off Tenerife at the time and we were pretty well provisioned – plenty of grog, plenty of food and the locals were friendly enough. So we didn't care too much; we knew he wouldn't be away long. It was only when he came back, came back without his men, alone and with a cut the size of a Turkish sabre across his head, that we realised what he'd done. He'd been off and buried his treasure and none of us knew where he'd hidden it.'

'Without his men? Do you mean he killed the men who helped him bury the treasure?' said Harriet.

Johnny nodded. 'That he did, the only safe way to keep the hiding place a secret. It meant that none of us knew where he'd buried it, so none of us could get our hands on the stuff.'

'That's why you betrayed him,' breathed Harriet, 'because he'd hidden his money, because he'd put it where you couldn't get your hands on it.'

In the darkness Johnny smiled. Harriet could see his golden tooth gleaming in the moonlight. He began to pace around the room and, slowly, his voice began to rise. 'It wasn't Bart's money, it was ours, mine as much as anyone's. We'd all worked for it, all of us, risking our lives day in, day out. What right did he have to go hiding it away?'

He paused and blew out heavily through his mouth. The action seemed to calm him. 'There was a map, of course – or, at least, rumours of a map.'

'Jethro's map,' Harriet whispered.

Johnny nodded. 'Aye, girl, Jethro's map, right enough. I knew that the map would give me the location of the treasure. And if anybody had that map, it would be old Jethro. Him and Jos Stephenson were the only ones close enough to Bart. He'd have confided in them. I couldn't get a sighting on Stephenson, dead most likely. But Jethro? Oh, I'd heard all about his comings and goings. Once I was released from Cape Corso, it was just a matter of tracking the old fool down.'

He turned to stare at Harriet. From outside the casement the day's first bird began to sing – dawn was not far away and Johnny Four Toes had clearly spoken for long enough. 'The map – get it!' he hissed.

At that moment there was a sudden sound from

downstairs. It might have been a log falling from the long dead fire or her father turning over in bed. Harriet did not care. Johnny Four Toes swung around towards the door and she seized her chance. In an instant she was out of bed, grabbing her dress in one hand and the corner of the casement in the other. Quickly and easily she swung up onto the ledge and dropped onto the ground outside. She landed with a bang that shook all the teeth in her head and fell forward onto the grass.

'Damn you, girl!' she heard Johnny curse and then she was up onto her feet and racing away into the night.

From the cottage behind her she heard a shout and, glancing quickly back over her shoulder, saw the pirate poised in the open casement. Even as she watched, he dropped into the darkness and Harriet lost sight of him. She sped like a gazelle across the green and into the undergrowth beyond, hardly knowing where she was going. Branches whipped across her face, but she kept running, away from the village and away from Johnny Four Toes.

Once she paused, listening for the sound of pursuit. She could hear nothing but knew that he was still coming after her. She quickly pulled on her dress, over her shift, then turned and ran once more.

When she came to a small valley, thickly shrouded by trees and bushes, it was even darker, the moonlight failing to penetrate the deep undergrowth. Silent shadows flitted from tree to tree and Harriet felt suddenly vulnerable. This was Squire Campbell's land and she knew that his house, the Court, was not far away. If she could just reach it, she thought, everything would be all right. Inside an hour the Squire would have his men out, combing the area and Johnny Four Toes would never get away.

She ran down the slope, across the brook at the bottom and started up the opposite incline. In the distance reared the dark bulk of the Squire's house and she knew that she had almost made it. At that moment she blundered into a dark shape that straddled and blocked the path. She opened her mouth to scream but strong arms enfolded her and a hand clamped firmly across her lips.

'Be quiet!' hissed the shape.

Harriet bit down hard on the hand that was gagging her. At the same time she kicked backwards with her foot, feeling a satisfying crunch as her heel connected with her captor's shinbone. She heard him curse softly. Then a blow caught her on the top of the head and sent her flying back into the undergrowth.

The next second Ben was at her side, whispering into her ear, 'Shh. Do you want to get us caught?'

Her mind whirling, Harriet lay on the cold earth, Ben's arm across her shoulder, and watched as Johnny Four Toes came into view. Like a nightmare creature, he scuttled along the path. Old Jethro had been right, Johnny limped heavily but it did not hinder his movements. The man was as agile as a monkey, swinging easily between the shadows and the shafts of moonlight that broke through the thick canopy of trees. Harriet and Ben shrank into the darkness as the pirate loped past them.

After a few moments Harriet heard Ben sigh and felt his body relax alongside her. 'What are you doing here?' she asked, her eyes still fixed on the point where Johnny Four Toes had disappeared into the night.

Ben grinned and rolled over onto his back.

'What do you think I'm doing? I'm after the Squire's rabbits. Well, I was until just now. Come to that, what are you doing here? Shouldn't you be tucked up in bed, out of harm's way?'

Harriet grimaced, sat up and began to brush the dirt off her dress.

Ben stared at her, expectantly. He had saved her life, there was no doubt about that, and Harriet knew she owed him some sort of explanation. He sat there, watching, eyes alive and questioning. She came to a quick decision. She couldn't do this on her own. And though Ben was only a year or so older, he was bigger and stronger than she was . . .

'Listen,' she said. 'I'll tell you everything. Then we can decide what we should do.'

They sat in the darkness of the woods and Harriet told her tale. She kept nothing back and Ben listened without interrupting.

Only when she had finished the story did he speak. 'I'd never have believed you if I hadn't seen Jethro with his throat cut. That map must be real. Otherwise Johnny would never take such risks. There's a fortune out there somewhere, waiting to be found. But we can't do this alone. We need to get some help.'

'Help from who?' Harriet asked. 'My father? Yours?'

Ben shook his head. 'The Squire. He's the only one who could mount an expedition – and that's what we need if we're going to find Black Bart's treasure.'

Harriet shook her head angrily. Already Ben was starting to take charge. What did he mean 'we'? It was her map, not his.

34

'No, listen, Harriet,' and Ben sounded more serious than she had ever heard him before. 'The Squire is the only one who can keep you safe from Johnny Four Toes. We've got to go and talk to him. And we've got to do it tonight before Johnny gets away. As long as he's on the loose, you'll never be safe.' He stood up and offered his hand to help Harriet up.

She sniffed and levered herself to her feet. 'I may be a girl, Ben Walters, but I'm not helpless.'

Cautiously, keeping a watchful eye for the desperate pirate, Ben and Harriet began to walk towards the Squire's house. Stackpole Court was shrouded in darkness. No lights were showing as they made their way down the long drive but as soon as Ben began to hammer on the oak door, dogs started to bark from somewhere inside. There was the sound of movement and soon a sleepy-eyed servant swung open the door.

'We need to see the Squire!' Ben demanded.

'Don't you know what time it is?' said the man. 'Go away and come back in the morning.'

He began to close the door in their faces but Ben was too quick for him and pushed his foot and arm into the open gap. Forcefully, he shouldered his way into the hall. Harriet pushed her way in behind him.

'We need to see the Squire now,' she said.

Three more servants silently appeared, standing in a line across the hallway, and Harriet began to think their mission had failed at the very first hurdle. At a signal from the first servant, the men began to inch forward, forcing the two youngsters back towards the door.

'What is it, Chambers?' called a voice from high above them.

35

Harriet glanced up and saw the tall figure of Squire Campbell standing at the balustrade. He wore a dressing gown and his fair hair, normally hidden beneath a wig or hat, was dishevelled and out of place.

'Two children, sir,' said the man called Chambers. 'From the village, I think.'

The Squire came slowly down the staircase and paused to squint at the intruders. He narrowed his eyes, searching his memory in order to put names to faces.

'It's Harriet, isn't it? John Amos's girl? And Ben Walters from the Customs and Excise Cottages. Been out after my rabbits again, eh, Ben? Well, come in the pair of you, come in.'

He waved the servants aside and watched as Chambers grumbled his way back to the pantry. Then he ushered them into a room leading off the main hall. It was filled with books. Harriet had never seen so many in one place and even Ben stopped and stared. Squire Campbell, however, was firm and keen to know their business.

'Well, now, what is it that makes you disturb a man's sleep in the middle of the night? Come on, let's have the story.'

They sat behind one of the tables and told their tale, starting with their meeting with Jethro and the map of Black Bart's island and treasure. After a few moments the Squire held up his hand to stop them. 'You say you have this map, Harriet?'

She nodded. 'Yes, sir, hidden in my bedroom. I can fetch it if you like.'

The Squire shook his head. 'That won't be necessary just yet. Wait a moment.' He reached out and pulled on a braided rope that ran down from the ceiling. From far away in the house they heard the sound of a bell ringing and, within a few minutes, Chambers ghosted in through the doorway. 'Wake Mr Lort, would you, Chambers. I think this is something he should hear.'

He waited until the old man had left the room and then turned to Harriet and Ben once more. 'We'll wait a few moments, if we may. There doesn't seem a lot of point repeating the story two or three times.'

Harriet felt Ben grow suddenly tense at her side and knew what he was thinking. The longer they delayed, the less chance there would be of capturing Johnny Four Toes. Yet the Squire had some reason for asking for this Mr Lort to join them. He was in control now and they had no option but to sit and fume and wait. Five minutes later the man in question came in through the door. Like the Squire he wore an expensive gown over his nightclothes but whereas Squire Campbell was tall and fair, this man was short and dark.

'What the devil is all this about?' he demanded. 'Don't you know the time, John? It's barely half past four.'

Squire Campbell held up his hand to pacify the man. Then he turned to Ben and Harriet once more. 'This is my brother-in-law, Nicholas Lort,' he said. 'As you can see, he is not an early riser. Now you can start your tale again, Harriet.'

Nicholas Lort threw himself down into one of the deep armchairs alongside the window and stared at them. Instinctively, Harriet knew she did not like him. Nevertheless she began her story once more while Lort sat yawning, half-listening and more than half-asleep.

Only when she mentioned the name Black Bart did the man suddenly seem to wake up and pay attention.

'You bought this map?' he demanded. 'You bought Black Bart's map from the peddler?'

'Yes, sir, for ten shillings.'

From the corner of her eye Harriet could see the Squire smiling. Slowly, carefully, she continued with her tale. When she told of her flight through the woods, the Squire leaned forward eagerly, fists clenched with tension. 'So he's still out there, even now?' he said, indicating over his shoulder towards the woods. 'Where do you reckon he's headed, Lort?'

The dark man shrugged and rose to his feet. He stood looking out of the window, seeing nothing. Even to Harriet and Ben it seemed as if he was trying to hide his excitement. Dawn was beginning to break, Harriet noticed, long slivers of grey mist creeping across the lawns and shrubbery of the great house.

'If this girl is right and he's a sailor,' said Lort, 'then he'll probably head back to sea. That's where he'll feel safest and that's where he'll be hardest to find. It's what I would do. The word is there's been a strange lugger moored off Freshwater East beach for the last few days. No-one seems to know where she's from. Could be connected, I suppose? Freshwater is the closest safe anchorage – after all, he'd hardly be likely to put in to Stackpole Quay, would he?'

Stackpole Quay was the Squire's own harbour, the place where the stone from his quarries was exported. He was on his feet now, his whole body active and alert. His eyes shone with excitement. 'Well, Lort, if this Johnny Four Toes had anything to do with the death of

38

the old peddler, then it's our duty to find out. Freshwater East may be our only lead. So that is exactly where I'm going. Are you coming with me?'

Lort shrugged but from the gleam in his eyes, Harriet knew that the man was far more interested in her map than he was in catching the killer of old Jethro.

Squire Campbell began bellowing orders and within five minutes the whole house was awake. Servants ran from one room to another, carrying clothes, pistols and food, and soon the sound of horses on the yard outside showed that almost every man from the estate had been roused.

'We'll need you to come with us, Harriet,' said the Squire, striding into the hallway. 'You'll have to identify this pirate when we spot him. Can you ride?'

'I can, sir,' said Ben. 'She can get up behind me.'

Harriet pushed down her impatience. Who did Ben think he was, telling Squire Campbell what she would do or not? She'd quite fancied galloping across the country on one of the horses from Stackpole Court stables. Now she would have to get up behind Ben, with him in charge – yet again.

Squire Campbell strode off to arrange for another horse. Harriet stood and watched. Everything seemed to be happening so fast, spiralling out of her control. *It's my map*, she thought to herself. What right did these people have to take control? Ben seemed to know what she was thinking and squeezed her arm, reassuringly, but she shrugged him away. He was as bad as anyone.

Soon everything was ready, a dozen horses snorting and filling the morning air with the sound of their stamping hooves and with the mist of their breath.

Squire Campbell had his plans already laid and pulled six of the biggest, strongest men to one side.

'Thomson, I want you to ride fast for Freshwater East,' he told their leader. 'Go across country and when you get there, set up a picket line across the road. The ford across the stream is the best place. Wait there until you hear from me or see me coming down the hill towards you. I'll take the coast road. We're going to flush this pirate out. We'll push him towards you, squeeze him between us so that he's got no place to run. Understand? Good, now go.'

Thomson smiled grimly and touched his forehead in salute. Then he turned and mounted his horse. The first party thundered away up the drive and the Squire glanced towards Harriet and smiled. 'We'll catch him, Harriet, never fear. Now, are you all ready?' He turned his horse's head and trotted almost casually away. Ben looked over his shoulder at Harriet, smiled in reassurance and began to follow the Squire down the road. The hunt had begun.

## Chapter Four

# The Chase

They galloped across the Squire's fields, the cold air of the early morning making Harriet shiver and hold tightly to Ben's back for warmth. The boy rode easily and well and had no difficulty in keeping up with the Squire and the others. All of the men, Harriet noticed, looked grimly determined and she was suddenly reminded of how dangerous this affair was likely to be. Johnny Four Toes had already killed once; he wouldn't hesitate to do it a second time.

'Keep your eyes open, everyone,' called the Squire as they crested the hill above the village. 'A guinea to the man who spots him first!'

With the sea on their right, the party spread out across the fields, moving forward at a steady trot. For perhaps twenty minutes they rode, none of them speaking or making a sound. Only the jangle of harness and the steady rumble of the horses' breathing disturbed the stillness of the morning air.

'This is stupid,' Ben muttered suddenly. 'What if Johnny Four Toes didn't come this way?'

'He must have,' said Harriet, shaking her head. 'Like Mr Lort said, Freshwater East is the best anchorage for miles around. And then there's the story of the lugger, remember? That's how he was planning to escape, I'm sure.'

Ben shrugged and glanced back at her. 'Maybe,' he said.

They lapsed into silence and rode steadily on across the hills and valleys. Escape or not, Harriet knew that sooner or later Johnny Four Toes would be back. He had come to find Black Bart's map and he hadn't got it. If she had read him correctly, he wasn't the type of man to give up at the first attempt. She knew he would be back.

The countryside out here, high above the sea, was greener than Harriet had imagined. She had never seen it from the back of a horse before and was surprised at just how beautiful it all was even in the grey light of early morning. Even so, it was hard to shake off a nagging sense of unease. She fidgeted, and started looking over her shoulder, moving awkwardly on the pony's back and causing it to stumble.

'Take it easy,' said Ben. 'You'll have us off in a minute. What's the matter?'

'I don't know.' Harriet found it hard to put her thoughts into words. 'I just get the feeling somebody's watching us.'

'Don't be foolish. Not even Johnny Four Toes would be that stupid. We're hunting him, remember?'

Harriet said no more, and Ben urged the pony to a steady trot.

After an hour or so the party began to move downhill, through the tiny hamlet of East Trewent, with its farm and whitewashed outbuildings. The huge bulk of Trewent Point lay out on their right.

The Squire eased his horse to a slow walk and scanned the horizon. 'Keep looking,' he called.

Harriet turned her gaze from the farm outbuildings,

towards a long line of hedgerow running down the side of a field of barley. Her eyes stung from lack of sleep and the effort of constant looking. She blinked, stifling a sudden yawn. She rubbed her eyes, then blinked them wide open to focus once more on the distant hedge. The ditch below was in deep shadow, a pool of darkness.

A sudden flight of gulls screaming overhead made her look up. What had startled them? Something flickered in the corner of her gaze, the tiniest of movements. Something, or someone, was stirring in the shadows of the hedge. For a second she froze. She didn't want to make a fool of herself in front of the Squire or Mr Lort.

No, there it was again, she was sure, that same flicker of movement. Perhaps it was a bird or a rabbit. Ben would laugh at her if it was. Harriet waited.

The third time she was certain. She jerked her head up in alarm. There wasn't a moment to lose. 'There!' she shouted, pointing. 'It's him!' And suddenly the small dark figure of the pirate was racing hell for leather down the line of the hedgerow.

A pistol cracked and Harriet saw a spurt of earth kick up in front of him. Fists clenched and body rigid, the figure faltered momentarily, then away he went once more, diving through a gap onto the road beneath. The roar of Lort's pistol shattered the morning air and Harriet heard and felt the whine of the ball as it shot past her cheek.

A sudden shout from the direction of the cliff top made them all look up: no sign of the fugitive, but Thomson and the remainder of the Squire's advance party marching up the hill towards them. 'He's making for the cliff, Squire. He's making for the Point!'

The riders dismounted swiftly, scrambled up the bank and stood staring at the headland that reached out like a giant finger into the sea. The land in front of them rose sharply for about a quarter of a mile, a grassy expanse that finally crumbled and fell away into a jumble of rocks at the far end. To left and right of the promontory the sea gleamed a dull pewter.

Johnny Four Toes was already well ahead of them, racing across the short springy turf. Not for the first time Harriet wondered at his speed – she would have been hard pressed to keep up with him.

'We've got him cornered,' shouted the Squire. 'There's no escape from up there. Spread out and move slowly.'

They advanced carefully onto the headland. Glancing to her right, Harriet thought that the long line of men could so easily have been beaters on one of the Squire's shoots, pushing the game before them onto the guns of the waiting hunters. Except that this time the quarry wasn't pheasants or rabbits. It was a man.

Slowly, inevitably, they closed in. Despite herself, Harriet almost felt sorry for him, running for his life, knowing that there was only one way this hunt could end. And then she remembered old Jethro lying dead under the hedge and her compassion faded. The pirate deserved everything he got.

Johnny Four Toes had reached the end of the headland and stood at bay, knife in hand and his back to the sea. The hunters pulled up ten yards in front of him, a long line of men stretching across the neck of the Point and cutting off his escape. All of them were breathing heavily, Harriet noticed, all but Johnny Four Toes.

'Give yourself up,' said the Squire. 'You've got nowhere to run. Give yourself up and come with us quietly. You'll get a fair trial, I promise you that.'

Johnny smiled unpleasantly. 'A fair trial? Like they gave me at Cape Corso? I don't think so.' His gold tooth gleamed and Harriet felt the fear turn over in her stomach. Johnny stared at her, ignoring the Squire and Nicholas Lort. When he spoke, it was to her. 'Well, girl. You fair ran old Johnny down. But it's not the end of the voyage, remember that, not by a long shot. Nothing's over till you're all tied up, shipshape and Bristol fashion alongside the quay. And this cruise has still got a long way to run.'

He glanced behind him. The sea hundreds of feet below was sullen, and dark shapes showed where wicked rocks lay beneath the surface. Johnny half-turned to face his captors, smiled once more, and then, with a sudden convulsive twist, he was gone.

Harriet watched in horror as he fell, arms and legs spread-eagled, through the air. Just before he hit the water, his body seemed to straighten and there was barely a splash as he entered the sea. For a moment there was no sign of him and Harriet began to think he must have been killed. Then, suddenly, Ben pointed and shouted, 'Look! There he is.'

A small dark shape had appeared in the water, thirty or forty yards beyond the cliff. Even as they watched there came a swirl of foam as Johnny struck out, swimming powerfully away from land.

'Shoot!' cried Nicholas Lort. 'Shoot him.'

A ragged volley rang out but Johnny Four Toes was already beyond pistol range and the shots fell harmlessly into the sea. And then, from under the lee of the headland, came the splash of oars. It was a longboat, powered by half a dozen burly sailors, moving swiftly through the water.

'Where the hell did that come from?' said Lort.

'Damn and blast him!' cursed the Squire. 'He's going to get away.'

They watched, helplessly, as the boat hove to alongside the swimming man. Within seconds Johnny Four Toes was on board, standing erect in the stern sheets, wiping the moisture from his face. He raised his arm and waved once to the men on the cliff top, then the longboat swept out to sea. On the horizon Harriet saw the low sleek shape of the mysterious lugger, already moving in to meet the pirates.

'Let's get back,' sighed the Squire. 'There's nothing more we can do here. We'll call at your father's Custom Station, Ben, but I doubt if they'll be able to do much, either. By the time they put to sea, those pirates will be long gone.'

Despondently they trooped down the headland and reclaimed their horses. It was a long and bitter ride back to Stackpole and nobody felt much inclined to talk. Only once, as they crested the rise above the village, did Nicholas Lort break the silence. 'At least we're free of him,' he said. 'We gave that pirate one serious fright. He won't be back here in a hurry.'

Something inside her told Harriet that he was wrong. She knew that Johnny would not give up so easily. At some stage he would be back, of that she was sure.

They called at the Customs cottages and alerted Ben's father, then watched as the crew of the cutter boarded their vessel and put out to sea.

'Now for the map, Harriet,' said the Squire. 'We'll pick it up from your cottage and take it to the Court for safe keeping.' They rode across the green and drew up outside the cottage door. Harriet's parents came out to greet them, her mother anxiously twisting her apron in her fingers, her father blustering.

'Where the devil have you been?' he demanded, glaring at her and ignoring the Squire.

Harriet looked at their pale and anxious faces. They had received only a brief message from the Squire in the middle of the night, telling them that their daughter was safe and was helping him in an important task. Now her father's face was white with anger and Harriet was suddenly glad that the Squire was there with her.

'You fetch the map,' said Squire Campbell. 'I will explain to your mother and father and tell them what's been happening.'

As she pulled the small oilskin packet from its hiding place alongside her casement window, Harriet could not help feeling bitter. This had been her secret, her dream, and now everyone seemed to be after a share of the spoils.

\*       \*       \*

'Cheer up, Harriet,' said Ben as they rode on to the Squire's house. 'If Black Bart really did sink all those ships, there'll be enough treasure there for everyone – more than you could spend in a whole lifetime.'

Reluctantly, Harriet agreed. 'I know,' she said, 'but it's not just that.'

When she thought about it logically, it wasn't the thought of sharing the money that was troubling her at all. Losing control of everything, seeing other people like the Squire and that man Lort pushing their way into her adventure, her vision and her dream, that was far more annoying.

And then, sitting there on the back of the Squire's horse, with the reassuring bulk of Ben's body in front of her, a much more worrying notion forced its way into her imagination. She shivered and glanced around urgently as a cold chill ran up her back. There was nothing to see but the old feeling of fear, the sense of being watched, had returned. And this time it was not just a vague notion. This time she was certain – from the woods or from the hills around the village, somewhere, somehow, somebody was watching them.

## Chapter Five

# About Black Bart

'Now then,' said the Squire, 'let me see the map.'

They were sitting, once more, in the library with sunlight streaming in long golden shafts through the windows. It was as if their adventures of the previous night, the flight through the woods and the manhunt up on Trewent Point, had never happened. They had breakfasted on coffee and fine white bread and the Squire and Nicholas Lort had changed out of their riding clothes. Yet Harriet felt out of place in the quiet room, sitting alongside Ben on a divan. She held the oilskin package firmly in her hands and knew that she was not yet ready to give it up.

'Didn't you hear the Squire?' Lort's voice was cold. 'Hand it over, girl.'

His eyes gleamed greedily and the old dislike surged up once more in Harriet's chest.

The Squire moved forward. 'Wait, Nicholas. This girl has done us a great service, the boy too. They don't need to be bullied.' He turned towards Harriet. 'What is the matter, my dear? We won't steal the map from you. You have nothing to fear from us. What can we do to help, Harriet? You do know what you've got there, do you not?'

Harriet clutched the oilskin packet to her chest. 'Yes, sir, it's Black Bart's treasure map.'

The Squire nodded. 'That's right. But what do you know of Black Bart?'

'Not much,' Harriet admitted. 'I know he was a pirate.'

'Not just any old pirate, Harriet, he was the greatest pirate who ever lived and he came from our county, our small part of Wales. Mr Lort, here, is an expert on the man. He's spent ten years researching his life and career, finding out all about him. No man alive knows more about Black Bart than my brother-in-law.'

He paused. 'Would you like to know more about him, Harriet?' The girl nodded, eager for information. 'Then Mr Lort will tell you. And after that, perhaps you will be more inclined to share your map with us.' He turned and inclined his head towards his brother-in-law.

Lort leaned forward. 'Like the Squire says,' he began reluctantly, his voice gruff with suppressed anger, 'Black Bart was a great pirate – if you can use a word like "great" when talking about thieves and cut-throats. His real name was John Roberts but he took the name Bart after he turned buccaneer. He went to sea when he was just thirteen years old but in 1719 when he was serving as Third Mate on the *Princess of London*, his ship was captured by Howell Davis, the pirate.'

'Another Pembrokeshire man,' said the Squire, 'and he offered Bart the chance to go on the account with him. That means . . .'

'I know,' said Harriet. 'Old Jethro told me.'

'It wasn't unusual in those days,' said Lort, warming to his tale, 'to go on the account like that. Lots of pirates took to the trade after being captured. Often it was a case of becoming a pirate or taking a musket ball to the brain. I'm not sure it was like that with Bart. He made a conscious choice to go on the account and they were pleased to have him, too. Well, he was a skilled navigator and knew how to handle men. He was in the slave trade at that time, running cargoes from the west coast of Africa to the Caribbean and at best he could expect to earn £3 a month. He had no chance of promotion and conditions on board those ships were terrible, even for the crew. But life as a pirate? It meant as much money as he could count and freedom to do as he wanted with his life. Anything was possible.'

'So he became a pirate for the money?' said Harriet.

Lort nodded. 'Why else? At the end of the day pirates want money. And when Howell Davis was killed, the men voted Bart as their leader. He didn't have much experience as a pirate but he was such a good sailor and navigator that they thought he was the best man for the job. And wasn't he just! He only lasted three years but in that time it's calculated that he took between 400 and 500 prize ships. Can you imagine that? More prizes than any other pirate who ever lived. For a while he almost brought transatlantic shipping to a halt – everyone was too frightened to put to sea. Just think of the treasure he must have taken in those three years.'

He paused and stared for a moment at the package that Harriet still held tightly to her chest. Slowly, he moistened his lips. 'Nobody has ever found all the gold and silver he took from those ships. Captain Ogle, who tracked him down and killed him, found some gold dust on his ship, the *Royal Fortune*, and a few coins but of the real treasure – and there must have been thousands and thousands of pounds' worth – nobody has ever seen a thing. There's never even been a hint, until now.'

Squire Campbell leaned forward and placed his hand on Harriet's knee. He squeezed gently and smiled at her.

'So you see why your map is so important, Harriet? This could make us all very, very rich. You need us to mount the expedition; we need you to give us the map.'

Harriet knew that the Squire spoke the truth. There was no way she could search for the treasure on her own. She needed the Squire for his men and his money and she needed this Nicholas Lort for his knowledge of Black Bart. She would have to trust them. Reluctantly, hesitantly, she passed across the oilskin packet. Eagerly, Nicholas Lort grabbed it and tore open the strings. Then he spread the parchment on the library table.

'Not much to go on, is there?' said the Squire, looking over Lort's shoulder. 'Where do you reckon it is?'

Harriet and Ben were beside him now, staring at the crudely drawn map.

Lort shrugged and frowned. 'I'm not sure. I must say it looks familiar but I'm damned if I can place it. They say Bart buried his treasure out near Africa but there's no latitude or longitude here to show the way.'

Something old Jethro had said came suddenly back to Harriet. 'No, sir,' she interrupted. 'It's not off Africa. Old Jethro said everyone thinks he buried his treasure at a place called Los Idols – or some name like that. But he said that Bart didn't. He said that he kept his gold much closer to home. And then he laughed, Jethro laughed, but I didn't know why.'

Lort nodded carefully.

Harriet looked at him and pointed to the map. 'There's some writing on the back. Maybe that will help.'

Lort turned the parchment over and stared at the poem that was written there. For two minutes he studied the words, concentrating hard, and then slowly he began to smile. He picked up the map and waved it in front of their faces. 'I've got it,' he exclaimed. 'I thought I recognised the place. I know where this is.'

Squire Campbell clutched at his brother-in-law's arm. Even Ben began to smile. Harriet felt her head whirling. If Lort really did know where the island was, then all the riches of the world would soon be at their feet.

'Look at the poem,' said Lort. 'It's all there. Flat Holm Isle is in the Severn Estuary, thirty or forty miles west of Bristol. *Ten paces from the mouth?* Easy. It's a cave; the treasure is buried in a cave.'

'On this Flat Holm Isle?' asked the Squire.

Lort shook his head and turned the parchment over once more. 'No. Look at the map. See the shape of the island? It's like a figure of eight – very distinctive. Look at the beach, the cliffs, the two hills – again, hard to mistake, as long as you know the place. And according to the poem, the cave is on an island just north of Flat Holm, facing due south. I know it, John, I've been there. I've sailed past it a dozen times. I've even landed there to take on water. It's no more than a hundred miles from this very spot where we're standing now.'

His finger jabbed down on the map and his face glowed with pleasure. 'No wonder Jethro said he kept his gold close to home. Everyone has been looking in the wrong place, in Africa and the Indies. But Black Bart fooled us all. He came home to bury his loot.'

Lort and the Squire threw their arms around each other and began to dance around the table. Then they seemed to remember their dignity and stopped, coughing and muttering. Ben grinned at them.

'But what is the House of Lords?' asked Harriet. 'It talks about them, there, in the poem.'

'Oh, that's nothing,' said Lort. 'The House of Lords was what they called the senior pirates, Bart's main advisors. It was a title they gave themselves. They had special privileges, and were even allowed ashore when they docked. They actually called themselves "My Lord" when they spoke to each other – delusions of grandeur if ever I heard it. The House of Lords was made up of men like Thomas Anstis and Joseph Stephenson. Oh yes, and John Jessup.'

'Johnny Four Toes,' said Harriet quietly.

Lort nodded and Ben came to her side and took her arm. He smiled, reassuringly.

Squire Campbell sat up suddenly and rested his chin in his hand. He closed his eyes and breathed out through his mouth, trying hard to contain his eagerness. 'You are sure about all this, Nicholas?' he said.

Lort nodded, hardly trusting himself to speak. The Squire glanced quickly at Harriet. 'And we do think the map is genuine, do we not?'

'Johnny Four Toes thought it was,' said Ben.

The Squire's head spun round and he stared at the boy for a few moments. Then he grinned. 'Then that's good enough for me. I'll have my yacht prepared and we can be at sea before you know it. Ben, you will be our cabin boy. I don't know if there is such a thing as a cabin girl, Harriet, but if there is then you can certainly be one. If not, we've just invented a new type of sailor.'

Even Nicholas Lort laughed. The Squire clapped them all on the back and rang for Chambers. He ordered sherry for himself and his brother-in-law, cups of hot chocolate for Ben and Harriet. Then they stood before the fireplace, discussing the expedition to come. Nicholas Lort, pleased with his deductions, was grinning from ear to ear and the Squire seemed to be filling the room with his laughter and enthusiasm.

Suddenly, however, Harriet froze, with her cup halfway to her mouth, and pointed to the window. 'Outside,' she whispered. 'There's a man.'

Everyone spun around, following the direction of her hand. The bushes beyond the gravel sweep of the driveway were tall and thick.

'Follow me!' ordered the Squire. He snatched up a heavy poker from the fire grate and ran to the hallway. Throwing open the front door, he raced across the grass, closely followed by Ben and Harriet. Lort came reluctantly behind, the map clenched firmly in his hand. They spent ten minutes searching through the under-growth. No-one.

'If there was anyone here,' said the Squire, 'he's long gone.'

'I know I saw someone,' Harriet said, close to tears. 'I didn't imagine it, sir, honestly I didn't.'

'Nobody is saying you did, child.'

From the look on Nicholas Lort's face, Harriet was not sure that everyone felt quite the same. They trailed back to the house, the Squire taking care to lock and bolt the front door behind them. Then he turned and took the parchment map from Lort's fingers.

'I think for the time being,' he said, 'that I had better take care of this. If that damned pirate has come back, we'd better not take any chances. For the next few days this map will not leave my side.'

Lort frowned. Harriet knew it was a wise precaution but something told her that the watcher, whoever he was, wasn't interested in the map. She couldn't explain her feeling. Squire Campbell saw her worried look and assumed she was concerned about the safety of the treasure. 'Don't worry,' he said. 'Nobody will get to the map. I'll have men posted around the house day and night and in a few days from now we will be at sea. The treasure is as good as ours already.'

The Squire was true to his word. A messenger was despatched to Pembroke, where the Squire's private yacht was lying, with orders that her captain should provision as quickly as possible and make sail for Stackpole Quay. Within a few hours the messenger had returned.

'The yacht will be ready in two days,' said the Squire to Harriet and Ben. 'In the meantime the pair of you had better stay here – at least that way we can keep an eye on you and know you're safe.' He walked away, whistling tunelessly to himself.

Even Ben seemed content, pleased at the thought of the cruise to come and to be staying for a while at the Squire's elegant house. 'We've beaten him, Harriet,' he said. 'We've beaten Johnny Four Toes at his own game. Nothing can stop us now.'

Then he wandered off to look at the shotguns in the Squire's gunroom. Yet something inside her told Harriet that things were very far from finished. Instinctively she knew that there would be danger and excitement in the days ahead, more danger than any of them had ever imagined. And she knew that very soon they would be seeing Johnny Four Toes again.

*Chapter Six*

# The Treasure Hunt

Harriet rested her arms on the bow rail of the Squire's yacht and watched the long Channel waves roll in towards her. They had been at sea for a day and a night and, according to Nicholas Lort, the island was now only a few hours away. Harriet had become used to the motion of the ship though at first she had felt sick and unsteady whenever the yacht dipped her bows into a breaker.

'Found your sea legs, eh, Harriet?' asked the Squire, coming up behind her.

'Yes, sir,' Harriet replied. 'It's lovely standing on board, watching the coast. It all looks so different.' She pointed towards the huge headland that was looming up on their larboard bow. 'I'm really enjoying it.'

'That's more than they are,' said the Squire, pointing to where Thomson and three of his men were perched precariously over the ship's stern. 'They've been ill since the moment we left Stackpole Quay.'

He turned back to gaze out over the bow. A fountain of spray and spume arched up beneath the bowsprit and the canvas above their heads billowed and snapped in the wind like a volley of musket shots. The yacht, *Caroline* as the Squire had christened her, was an American-built sloop, fore-and-aft rigged, as fast as any ship on the Welsh coast. Now, with all sails set, she was making excellent time.

'We should be off the island by nightfall,' said the Squire. 'Then tomorrow we'll be ashore and digging for gold. What do you say to that, eh?'

Harriet smiled and hugged herself, feeling that it was almost too good to be true. Then she caught a glimpse of Nicholas Lort, standing at the stern rail. She shivered, without really knowing why, and realised that the man had been observing her ever since they had set sail. It was disconcerting – why should he be watching her so closely? Ben came running along the deck to tell them that food was ready in the saloon and Harriet went down below, forgetting about the all-seeing eyes of Lort, knowing that their quest was almost over.

Six hours later, the yacht rounded the eastern point of the island and dropped anchor a few hundred yards off the beach, between the island and the mainland. Harriet had stood in the bows for most of the afternoon, watching as the tiny island materialized over the horizon. The cliffs on the southern side had looked formidable as the sloop sailed past the island in order to reach the anchorage, and the two hills stood out like sentry posts against the evening sky. She had tried to pick out the cave but already it was too dark to see more than shadows. The place was deserted and even the mainland, half a mile away, seemed devoid of life.

'Can we go ashore now?' Harriet asked.

The Squire shook his head. 'Too dangerous in this light, best wait for morning. This is a good, safe anchorage; we'll be fine here until tomorrow.'

Harriet slept little that night but spent the hours tossing and turning, restless as the sea itself. A million different thoughts and plans kept storming into her brain. She would buy a yacht like the Squire's, she decided, and sail around the world. She would build her parents a fine house. She would pay for Jethro to be properly buried in the churchyard.

Stifling a shout of impatience, she jumped out of her bunk and, in the darkness of the stern cabin, quickly pulled on the boy's clothes she had found there. She had discarded her dress the previous day, realising that breeches and a waistcoat were far more practical attire on board ship. Ben had stared at her in amazement when he had first seen how she was dressed.

Quietly, Harriet climbed the companionway to the main deck. There was almost no sound and barely a breath of wind. All that disturbed the silence was the lap of waves against the hull and the hollow guttering of the ship's stern lantern. To her surprise Harriet found that she was not alone. Nicholas Lort sat on the gunwale, staring at the dark bulk of the island that lay almost within touching distance. He was fully dressed and there were dark rings of tiredness beneath his eyes.

'I'm sorry,' said Harriet. 'I didn't mean to disturb you.'

Lort shrugged and turned away. He did not speak but yawned and stretched upwards to ease his neck and back. Harriet suddenly knew that the man had been up here all night, just sitting and watching. She glanced at the rapidly lightening eastern sky. A few pale strips of red had appeared further up the Channel and already the features of the island were beginning to take on distinctive shapes.

'Why?' said Lort suddenly, speaking as much to the empty deck as to her. 'Why doesn't everybody wake up and get started?'

Harriet stared at him. He had rarely spoken to her before, unless it was to answer a question or to make a demand. She seized her chance and sat alongside him on the rail. Lort sniffed and moved a few feet away. Harriet was not to be put off.

'Can I ask you about Black Bart, sir?' Harriet said.

'Very well, what do you want to know?' Lort's enthusiasm for the subject had got the better of him.

'I want to know how it all ended. Jethro said he was killed by grapeshot.'

Lort nodded. 'That's right. The pirates were surprised while they were anchored at a place called Parrot Island, off Cape Lopez. For your information, that's on the Guinea coast of Africa. Your friend Jessup – Johnny Four Toes as you call him – had turned traitor and told Captain Ogle where to find Bart's ship. Nobody knows why he did it – money and the King's pardon, I suppose. Anyway, most of the pirates were drunk or sleeping off hangovers so it was all over quite quickly. Bart Roberts took a shot to the throat and died instantly.'

He paused and stared towards the island. 'According to one story, his helmsman, Joseph Stephenson, saw Bart fall across a cannon. He shouted at him to get up and fight. Then he saw that Bart was dead and he broke down in tears. Stephenson loved Bart Roberts like a brother and went raging around the deck, swearing to get even with John Jessup if it was the last thing he ever did.'

'What happened to him, to Stephenson, I mean?'

Lort shook his head. 'How the Devil should I know? Nobody knows. His name didn't feature in any of the trial records so it's always been assumed he was killed in the battle and, like Black Bart, his body thrown over the side. But nobody knows for sure.'

There was a sudden commotion at the companionway hatch and Squire Campbell came bustling onto deck. 'A fine morning, Lort. Some breakfast, I think, then it's off to the island. There's a little matter of treasure waiting to be dealt with. What do you say, Harriet?'

Breakfast was a hurried affair and within the hour the *Caroline's* longboat was launched. Squire Campbell stood in the bows, issuing orders to the crew and to the estate workers he had brought with him. 'Another shovel, Thomson, and a pickaxe. Look lively, man, we want to be ashore today, not next week. And, Phillips, we'll have another cask of water.'

The longboat pulled easily away from the side of the yacht, turned its bow into the wind and headed for the island. A few minutes later it grounded on the sand and shingle of the beach. Ben was over the side in an instant, standing up to his waist in the water.

'I claim this island for Black Bart and all true venturers!' he shouted as he waded ashore.

Soon everyone had followed Ben's example. They pulled the boat up onto the beach and began to unload the supplies.

'We'll set up a camp above the tide line,' said the Squire. 'See to it, Thomson.' He turned to Nicholas Lort. 'Right, let's find this cave.'

Lort led the way to the eastern hillock. It was easy walking, the grass springy and soft beneath their feet. As they approached the hill, grass began to give way to rock and soon they were clambering over smooth slabs of limestone. At the extreme end of the island, where the rock face broke up into beds of scree and shale, Lort turned to the south. 'Just there,' he said and pointed.

Harriet squinted and eventually managed to pick out a darker shade of black against the rock, halfway down the face. The cave was hidden from the shore and even from anyone who chanced to walk that way. Only from the sea was it in any way visible – and even then you would have to know exactly where to look.

'We came ashore for water a few summers ago,' Lort explained. 'It was high tide and I found myself staring straight into the cave. Otherwise I'd never have known it was here.'

The Squire produced a rope and secured one end to a large boulder. 'It's the only way down, I'm afraid,' he said. 'Who wants to be first?'

Nicholas Lort and Ben climbed hand over hand down the rope and stood waiting at the cave mouth. When it came to Harriet's turn, she swung out over the drop and tried not to think about the jagged rocks that waited below if she should chance to slip or fall. Three seconds later she felt Ben's arms around her waist and was pulled onto the platform at the open mouth of the cave.

'Perhaps the trousers were a good idea, after all,' Ben said, laughing.

Harriet made a face at him and pushed his arm away as the Squire came sliding down the rope. Panting, he joined them at the entrance to the cave. Within a few moments one of the estate workers arrived with torches.

'Stand back,' said the Squire. He struck his flint and the first torch burst into flame. Soon, all three torches were burning brightly and the advance party followed the Squire into the darkness. The cave was long and smelled like the seaweed Harriet saw her father sometimes spread on his land as fertilizer. There was a constant drip of water and the noise of the waves crashing onto the rocks below seemed twenty times louder here than ever it did up on the cliff top.

'Ten paces from the mouth,' said Lort, breathlessly.

Carefully, with painstaking accuracy, he marked off the distance. Then he thrust his spade into the dirt floor. There was a hollow clang and he dropped the spade. 'Damnation! There's a rock or something here.'

The three men fell to their knees and scraped away the sand and dirt while Harriet and Ben held the torches. The boulder they uncovered was at least six feet in length and covered almost a third of the cave floor. 'It's like a lintel or a cap-stone,' said the Squire. 'It would take a hundred men to move it. God alone knows how Black Bart managed to put it there. There's only one way to get to the treasure – we'll have to dig underneath it.'

They stood and considered his words. None of them had expected the treasure to be just lying there but this was a difficulty nobody had foreseen. Digging beneath the boulder would be dangerous and time-consuming. For perhaps two minutes nobody spoke, then Nicholas Lort broke the silence. 'Well, the treasure's lain here for twenty years. It's not going to hurt for a day or so longer.'

The Squire raised his hand. 'We need to approach this methodically,' he said, probing the loose sand with the end of his stick. 'Or we'll end up burying ourselves in sand and shingle. We need someone who knows about these things.'

'What about John Thomson?' said Lort. 'He used to be a miner, didn't he?' It was true; the man had spent years underground, toiling at the Pembrokeshire coalface.

Thomson was called, but despite his help, the work was even harder than they expected. The roof of their excavation kept falling, trapping and covering the diggers in mounds of choking debris and they needed every spare bit of planking from the *Caroline* to shore it up. Under Thomson's direction they built a protective tunnel above their heads. For three days the Squire and his men worked.

\*      \*      \*

Each night they returned to the *Caroline*, leaving two men armed with muskets and cutlasses to mount guard. And each night the Squire fretted about the delays and problems. 'The longer we're here, the more attention we draw to ourselves,' he fumed.

But there was no alternative and so they dug on. None of them dared to admit, not even to themselves, the nagging doubts, the fear that maybe there was no treasure after all.

'Nothing,' cursed the Squire on the morning of the fourth day, 'not a sign of anything. No coins, no jewellery, nothing. There's not even any sign of digging. I'm beginning to doubt Black Bart was ever here.'

Nobody said a word but later that afternoon, sitting on top of the lookout point, Harriet wondered how long it would be before the search was abandoned.

They all took turns to keep watch. It was a task Harriet enjoyed, sitting up there in the fresh air, training her telescope on passing ships and imagining the exotic places they would soon be visiting. Parrot Island, Cape Lopez, the Guinea Coast of Africa – even the names were exciting. It was better than thinking about the others in the cave, stripped to the waist, toiling and sweating through another day of disappointment.

Suddenly a cry broke across her daydream. 'Harriet! Harriet!' She looked down towards the cave to where Ben was waving frantically up at her. 'We're in, Harriet!' he called. 'We're in! We need you!'

Harriet's heart leapt. She grabbed the rope and swung herself down the cliff face. Hardly pausing to regain her breath, she and Ben bounded into the cave. The place was illuminated by several torches pushed into cracks in the walls, the flames guttering and dancing in the breeze. They threw strange shadows onto the faces of the men who stood, dirty, exhausted and elated, around the chamber.

'Careful,' whispered the Squire, crawling out of the excavation and thrusting a torch into her hand. 'Go carefully, Harriet, but I think you're the only one small enough to get through.'

His eyes gleamed as he pushed her forward and Harriet crawled on hands and knees under the boulder. For ten feet she shuffled along, feeling as if the whole roof might collapse at any moment and bury her alive. Then suddenly and unexpectedly the tunnel seemed to open up and she almost fell into a large, echoing chamber. It was twenty or thirty feet wide and was perfectly symmetrical.

'It's hollow,' she whispered. 'The inside of the hill is hollow.'

She could see sheer walls soaring high above her head, tapering gently inwards and disappearing into the darkness beyond the range of the torch flame. She looked and for a moment her heart seemed to stop. She blinked, then wiped at her eyes, hardly able to believe what she saw in front of her. She stood up and walked into the middle of the cavern.

A dozen sea chests, all open and all full of gold and silver coins, stood ranged against the cavern wall. There were doubloons and guineas, coins from England, France and Portugal, every country in the world that had ever minted its own currency. Lying alongside and between the chests were bars of yellow gold and more heaps of coins. There were glittering rubies and green emeralds, necklaces and rings, tiaras and crowns, all shining and sparkling in the light of her single torch. It was the treasure of a great pirate, a treasure that had cost the lives of hundreds of men, honest sailors and pirates alike.

The Squire's muffled voice, calling anxiously from the tunnel entrance, brought her back to reality. 'Are you all right, Harriet?'

'Yes,' she called back. 'Come and see. There's more room than you think.'

Soon there was a clatter of boots on the cavern floor. Squire Campbell, Mr Lort and Ben gazed about them in wonder.

'Eight hundred thousand guineas if it's a penny,' whispered Lort, his voice echoing around the cavern.

'Welcome,' said the Squire, 'to Black Bart's treasure.'

*Chapter Seven*

# The Return of Johnny Four Toes

It took them three long days to transfer the treasure from the cave to the hold of the *Caroline*. It was hard, back-breaking work, hauling the boxes and chests up the sheer cliff face and then carrying them to the beach. Yet it was a task that nobody complained about or tried to avoid. As the Squire had said, everyone would share in the fortune and that helped the men to redouble their efforts.

'Difficult work, Harriet,' said the Squire, pulling up the slope towards the foot of the eastern hillock.

It was lunch time on the third day and Harriet was on her way to the beach with two bars of gold. They were heavier than she expected. She carried the gold ingots in a makeshift pannier, slung across her shoulders, the bar on one side balancing with one on the other.

'Take a break when you reach the beach,' continued the Squire, mopping his face and wiping away the sweat. 'Ben's there. He has bread and cheese and a little wine.'

Harriet watched him stride away back up the hill, then turned and slowly made her way to the beach. As the Squire had said, Ben was waiting for her, his back resting easily against the gunwale of the longboat. He had spent most of the morning rowing backwards and forwards between the *Caroline* and the shore, ferrying out boatloads of gold and silver. Like Harriet, he was tired and in need of a rest.

'Help yourself,' he said, indicating a wicker basket that sat on the sand. 'There's plenty.'

Harriet needed no second urging and it was the work of only minutes to demolish the bread and cheese. The sun was hot and the wine, even though it was well diluted with spring water, went quickly to her head. Soon she felt her eyes beginning to close.

'Take a nap,' said Ben. 'That's what I'm going to do – at least for ten minutes or so.'

Harriet lay back on the sand, her hands behind her neck, neatly pillowing her head. She was conscious of Ben's steady breathing as he lay alongside her – the boy had fallen asleep in seconds. The sun was warm, caressing her face and arms in a golden glow. Dreaming about the fortune that now nestled in the hold of the yacht, she fell asleep.

*          *          *

When she opened her eyes she thought for a moment she must still be dreaming – a nightmare, she was sure. Johnny Four Toes was standing in front of her. But when she saw that Ben was crouching next to her upon the sand, staring up in disbelief at the pirate, panic clawed at Harriet's chest. She scrabbled urgently to her feet.

'Easy, girl,' said Johnny, holding out his arm to calm her. 'I'm not going to hurt you.' He half turned and beckoned to the men who stood some way behind him. There must have been twenty of them, Harriet reckoned, all of them armed with muskets, pistols and cutlasses. A more villainous group of ruffians Harriet had never seen. Behind them she noticed the low shapes of two longboats rocking gently in the swell.

'Jeb,' said Johnny, 'take a dozen of the lads up to the top of that there hill. I want the Squire and his crew taken and brought back down here in five minutes flat.'

Jeb, a tall sailor with a tarred pigtail and a scar across his cheek, touched his fingers to his forehead and grinned. Harriet saw that there was more than a little mockery in the man's salute. She would remember it, she thought, store it away for future use.

'Dead or alive, Johnny?'

Johnny Four Toes shrugged. 'Can't say as I care that much.' He paused and turned to stare at Harriet and Ben. 'On second thoughts,' he continued, 'alive would probably be better – a lot less trouble all round.'

He watched as Jeb and his men doubled away up the beach and moved onto the grassy slope. Suddenly, without turning his head or moving a muscle in his body, he hissed out a command. 'Leave it, boy!'

Harriet's head shot around. Ben had been inching across the sand to the spot where his pistol lay alongside the lunch basket. At the sound of Johnny's voice, the boy started and dived for the weapon. Quick as a rattlesnake, Johnny Four Toes leapt forward and stamped down across Ben's arm. The boy cried out in pain but Johnny just ground down with his heel.

'No time for heroics, boy,' he hissed. 'I told you to leave it and I meant it. Do what I say and we'll get on well. Disobey and –'

He left the sentence unfinished but there was no mistaking the menace in his voice. He jerked his head and one of the remaining pirates stooped to pick up the pistol. Johnny took the gun, inspected it and then tossed it casually over his shoulder. With a dull, almost hollow splash, it fell into the water ten feet out from the shore. Ben sat back on the sand, ruefully rubbing at his arm.

Johnny was barefooted, Harriet noticed, like all of the men he had brought with him. She supposed that it was easier walking in bare feet when there was sand and water to deal with. Despite herself, she felt her eyes being drawn to Johnny's deformed foot, the first toe missing, the others crushed and mutilated.

'Not a pretty sight,' said Johnny, noticing the direction of her gaze. 'But it's all part of the risk when you become a gentleman of fortune.' He smiled at her. 'A cannon ball took off the toe in my very first battle, first time on the account. And Black Bart himself gave me my nickname – Johnny Four Toes. He meant it as a joke but for some reason it seemed to stick and that's what I've been called ever since.'

He fixed one of the remaining men with a steel-hard gaze and jerked his head in the direction of the Squire's yacht. 'Your turn, Tom,' he said.

The pirates moved to one of the longboats and within moments had pushed off from the beach. Now only Johnny was left standing in front of Harriet and Ben. Carefully, he pulled a pair of double-barrelled pistols from his waistband and drew back the hammers.

'How did you get here?' Harriet managed to splutter, finding her voice at last.

Johnny shrugged. Behind him the longboat bumped gently into the side of the *Caroline* and the pirates swarmed on board. 'We followed you up the coast. It seemed the sensible thing to do once you'd run me off that headland – well, you had the map and I thought it was as well to let you do the treasure hunting. We were a few hours behind you all the way.'

He threw back his head and laughed, his gold tooth flashing in the afternoon sunshine. 'We've been watching you. Why bother breaking our backs? I thought, let them do all the work. So we sat in comfort on the lugger and watched and waited while you very generously moved Black Bart's gold for us. When the job was almost over, I thought it was time to take a hand.'

Harriet gazed around, trying hard to pick out the low sleek shape of Johnny's lugger. It had to be here somewhere, she thought. As if he could read her mind, Johnny Four Toes shrugged his broad shoulders. 'Oh, the ship's not here; she's moored a few miles down the coast. We came by longboat, much quieter all round, much less likely to be spotted by anyone who happened to be keeping watch.'

He turned to gaze out at the yacht and at that moment a scream echoed across the water. It was a drawn-out cry of agony. Harriet felt the hairs on the back of her neck stand up like a line of soldiers. All along the island startled sea birds rose, flapping and calling into the air. Harriet knew that one of the Squire's men had resisted and paid for it with his life.

'You butcher!' she cried.

Johnny said nothing. He seemed to be waiting for something else. And then the sudden boom of musket shots reverberated from beyond the eastern hill. Once, twice, three times, the guns fired. Then silence.

'Stupid,' said Johnny Four Toes, 'really stupid. They should have realised that Jeb would as soon kill them as bring them back alive. Now me, I don't believe in wasting life, not even your Squire's,' he paused, 'unless there's no other way.'

Harriet's heart was heavy. Had the Squire and Mr Lort been killed? It was too desperate a thought to consider. Presently, however, Jeb's party began to straggle back over the crest of the hill, pushing and prodding the Squire, Lort and two others in front of them. Of Thomson, the hero of the excavation, there was no sign.

'How many?' asked Johnny as the group came padding across the shingle.

Jeb shrugged. 'Just two. Two as felt they ought to protect their investment.'

Angrily the Squire turned on him. 'Cold-blooded murder, that's what it was. I'll see you hanged and drying in the sun on Execution Dock if it's the last thing I ever do.'

Jeb shrugged, nonchalantly. Then his pistol swung suddenly upwards through the air, the butt smashing into the Squire's skull. Harriet gasped as the Squire fell to the sand, blood spurting from the wound.

'The last thing you ever do?' said Jeb. 'Don't worry about that, my friend, I'll make sure it doesn't come to that.' He moved forward, pistol levelled, but Johnny raised his hand and stilled him with a glare.

'Leave it, Jeb. We've more important business.'

Cursing under his breath, Jeb lowered his pistol as Lort helped the Squire to his feet. Out in the anchorage the longboat pushed off from the side of the *Caroline*. Soon it had grounded on the shingle and the yacht's captain and two seamen were herded up the beach towards them.

'All secure?' asked Johnny.

Tom nodded. 'One man tried to make a run for it. He won't do it again.'

'And the treasure?'

'All there,' said Tom. 'Every last ounce of gold, every doubloon and guinea Black Bart ever took; all his pieces of eight, all his silver. It's all ours.'

Nicholas Lort could contain his fury no longer. 'It's not yours, damn your eyes! It's ours. We found it; we brought it here out of the cave. You've got no right to that treasure, none at all.'

Jeb's pistol came up, the barrel jabbing viciously into Lort's throat. 'Another move and you're a dead man!'

Lort pulled up short. Johnny Four Toes frowned at him and, carefully, un-cocked his pistols. He handed them to one of the pirates and moved to within an inch of Lort's face. He spoke quietly, his words full of malice. 'No right? Man, who do you think took that treasure in the first place? Not Black Bart, that's for sure. He just stood around in his fancy red coat, throwing out orders. No, we took that gold. What you see in front of you here is all that's left of Bart Roberts's crew. Twenty of us, that's all, out of over three hundred. We fought for that gold and many died for it. Nobody has more right to it than us.'

He drew back his hand and for a moment Harriet thought he would strike Lort. But Johnny simply waved dismissively, and turned to Jeb.

'The captain of the yacht,' he said. 'Deal with him.'

Jeb instantly whirled around, cutlass flashing. The yacht's captain uttered not a sound but fell, stone dead, upon the sand. Harriet screamed.

'Confound you, man,' cried the Squire. 'What sort of animal are you?'

Johnny shrugged. 'A desperate one, Squire. That man was a sailor. You, on the other hand, are just amateurs. As long as he was alive you had a chance of getting yourself another ship and following us. Think of it this way – he died so that you can live. Surely there's no greater sacrifice than that? As it stands now, you're stuck here, marooned on this island. This way I don't have your blood on my hands.'

Sick as she was in her heart and stomach, Harriet knew the man spoke the truth. It wasn't compassion or care about their safety. He was just being practical. The Squire had too many powerful friends, people who would come looking for justice should anything happen to him.

'Time to go,' Johnny said, suddenly. Then he turned to face Harriet and Ben. 'And we'll take this pair with us.'

The shock of his words was like a wall of cold water being poured over their heads. Harriet felt her stomach lurch; the colour drained from Ben's face.

'Good God, man,' shouted the Squire. 'Why? They're just children. They're no use to you.'

'Hostages, Squire,' said Johnny. 'Who knows, you might just manage to get yourselves off this island and decide to come after us. My advice to you is simple – don't. You know what will happen to your young friends if you do.'

'Bad luck to take kids like that,' said Jeb suddenly, his eyes unhappy and unsure. 'I ain't ever seen no good come out of bringing kids on a cruise.'

Johnny glared at him. 'Trust me, Jeb. We need those

74

youngsters. They'll be worth their weight in gold.' He grinned and said no more. The silence spoke volumes.

A flurry of activity broke out as the pirates pushed Harriet and Ben into one of the longboats, then crowded in behind them. Johnny Four Toes was the last. 'Thank you, my friends,' he called. 'A good day's work, I think.' He laughed and the sound echoed like a peel of doom around the bay. He pulled his mutilated foot over the gunwale of the boat and stared ahead to where the elegant shape of the Squire's yacht swung easily at her cable.

'You'd leave us here?' shouted Lort. 'Leave us here without food and water?'

Johnny turned in his seat and spread his hands. 'I leave you as I found you,' he shouted back. 'Not wealthier, perhaps, but wiser, certainly wiser. For myself, I leave laden with riches.'

And guilt, Harriet thought, more guilt than any one man should ever have a right to earn. She felt sick with fear and sadness. So many men had died in the hunt for Black Bart's treasure. She knew that she and Ben were in danger. It would not take much for Johnny Four Toes or one of these murderous pirates to stick a knife in their ribs.

As the longboat pulled towards the *Caroline,* Harriet cast a quick glance back towards the forlorn figures on the island. They were still standing on the beach, gazing helplessly after the departing boats. As she watched, the Squire raised his hand.

Johnny Four Toes saw the gesture, too. 'Marooned and left without their treasure, eh? What a cruel thing fate is.' He smiled at her and Harriet knew that, when he smiled like that, the man was at his most dangerous.

The longboat swept alongside the *Caroline* and Harriet and Ben were pushed roughly on board. Then the pirates set about the process of getting the yacht ready for sea. Johnny Four Toes stood on the quarter deck, eyes fixed firmly on the mainland.

'What is it?' asked Jeb as he took his place at the tiller.

Johnny shrugged. 'I'm not sure, there's something not quite right. I don't know what it is, all I know is I've got a mighty strange feeling in my water.'

Jeb stared at him, his face puzzled and unsure. 'What sort of feeling?'

Johnny's eyes had not left the shore line. He seemed to be searching for something. 'I can't rightly place it,' he said. 'I feel we're being watched – and I don't mean by them dogs back on the island, either. Yes, that's it. Somebody is watching us.' He glared around the deck and his gaze fell on Harriet and Ben. 'Move those damned kids down below!' he shouted. 'And run up the Jolly Roger!'

As the flag was hoisted to the masthead, Harriet and Ben were hustled below deck. Despite the danger, Harriet could hardly restrain a smile. She had been having exactly the same feeling as the pirate. Suddenly she knew that the hidden watcher, whoever he was, spelt as much danger to Johnny Four Toes as he did to her. She felt better immediately.

## Chapter Eight

# The Point House

Harriet and Ben were bundled below deck and locked into one of the small cabins next to the hold. There they had the torment of knowing that the treasure they had laboured so long to uncover and carry from the cave lay only a few feet away. And yet it was as far beyond their reach as if it had been buried on some distant isle in the Spanish Indies.

Within a few minutes of the key being turned in the cabin door, they heard the thunder of feet on the deck above their heads as the pirates ran to man the capstan bars. Listening carefully, they even managed to pick out the combined intake of breath as the crew drove the bars forward. Then came the creak of the cable as the anchor slowly freed itself from the seabed and snaked its way on board. Finally, the *Caroline* gathered way and they were off.

\*       \*       \*

'What do you think will happen to the Squire and the others?' asked Harriet. She was lying on the bunk, listless and preoccupied. She and Ben had spoken hardly a word to each other as the *Caroline* cut into the swells of the Severn Estuary. Yet she was keenly aware that the motion of the sea had increased over the past few hours – it was going to be a rough night.

Ben shook his head. 'I should think they'll be all right. The first passing ship will probably lift them off and take them into Swansea. They might have to wait a day or so but at least they'll be safe back there, which is a hell of a lot more than can be said for us.'

Harriet knew the boy spoke the truth. Once Johnny Four Toes and his gang were safely out of the danger zone, well away from the Squire and his friends, then they would not need the security of hostages. Ben's life, and hers, would be worthless, of that she was sure.

The yacht suddenly pitched into a heavy swell, the movement making Harriet cling to the side of her bunk for safety. She glanced at Ben, eyes questioning. 'She certainly buried her bows into that one,' she said.

Ben nodded grimly but said nothing and lay back on his bunk. The night wore on, the yacht battered and tossed around like a cork in a bowl of water. The *Caroline* was built for speed, not for fighting heavy seas like this, and even a novice sailor could sense that she was making heavy weather of the voyage.

Harriet lay and tried to work out what she felt. Fear? Yes, she was afraid. She did not want to die. But there was something more, the feeling that, by her actions, by her enthusiasm for the quest, she had unleashed a force that would grow and grow until it had consumed everything in its path. Whatever it was, it was vicious and evil and she had brought it to life.

Eventually Harriet fell into a restless sleep. When she awoke a few hours later, dawn was breaking and she could feel that the motion of the ship had changed. She was still rocking and lurching in the swell but now she was not ploughing forward into the breakers. The yacht had come to a stop. Ben was already on his feet, peering out of the starboard scuttle.

'We've hove-to alongside their lugger,' he declared.

Harriet pushed her way to the porthole. The boy was right. The low sleek shape of the lugger was hard up alongside their starboard bow and, gazing over her deck towards the shore, Harriet could see that they were lying off a small inlet. She did not recognise the place. Even as they watched, three pirates clambered across the gap between the two vessels. A few minutes later came the sound of hammering and soon the lugger began to settle gently by the bows.

'They've stove in her planking,' said Harriet. 'Getting rid of the evidence, I suppose. And they really don't need her now that they've got the *Caroline*.'

The lugger sank easily and elegantly. Soon, only her single mast was visible above the shallow water. Within minutes the *Caroline* had gathered way again.

A sudden bang from the door brought their heads around. Jeb stood in the cabin threshold. 'Johnny says you're to come on deck,' he growled. 'No nonsense or I'll batter your brains in myself.'

A thin unpleasant drizzle had begun to fall and the deck as they came up the companionway was slippery and dangerous. They found Johnny Four Toes at the stern of the yacht, watching as the coast and the mast of the lugger, still pointing upwards from the sea like an admonishing finger, disappeared over the horizon. The man seemed to have recovered some of his good temper.

'Welcome,' he beamed, as if he was the Squire himself, throwing open the deck of his ship to casual visitors. 'Make yourselves at home.' Then he grinned but, somehow, the smile failed to work and turned, instead, into a grimace. 'After all, you're not going far.'

'But where are we going?' asked Ben.

Johnny Four Toes glanced over his shoulder, back in the general direction of the island. 'West,' he said. 'Back to Pembrokeshire.'

Harriet could hardly believe her ears. 'That's stupid. It's the first place the Squire will look. That's where he'll be heading as soon as he gets off the island.'

Johnny nodded. 'Indeed. But he won't be leaving the island in a hurry. And by the time he does, we'll have finished our business and be away. If by some miracle he gets ashore, he's got no ship and so he'll have no choice but to go by road. And that is a very slow way to travel, very slow indeed.'

Harriet shook her head. It seemed to be a foolhardy thing, this returning to Pembrokeshire. But she was not about to argue with the pirate. It was his funeral, she thought.

Yet again Johnny seemed to anticipate her. 'We need to victual the ship. It's a long haul across the Atlantic, even in a fast vessel like this. And there's only one place to stock up with supplies for gentlemen of fortune like us.'

Something her father had said a week or two before seemed to resurface in Harriet's brain. 'The Point House Inn?' she said. 'At Angle?'

Johnny Four Toes nodded and stared at her with new respect. 'Well, girl, I'm almost inclined to say you'd make a good pirate. Black Bart would have been proud of you.'

Harriet opened her mouth to respond but the *Caroline* bit deeply into a breaker and a wave of swirling water came surging along the deck. Johnny Four Toes turned towards Jeb and Tom. 'Let's get some lines rigged up across the deck. There's plenty of bad weather ahead, I should say.' He turned back to Harriet and Ben. 'And you two had better get below again. You'll be a lot less bother down there.'

For the next few hours the *Caroline* pitched and rolled her way across Carmarthen Bay, fighting the giant rollers that pounded in from the Atlantic. Harriet lay on her bunk and dozed. The motion of the yacht did not bother her but she knew that she had to find a way of stopping Johnny getting away with the treasure. She didn't know how but she did know that she had to do something.

'Penny for your thoughts,' said Ben at last.

It was early afternoon and the sea seemed to have calmed a little. Like Harriet, Ben was lying on his back, wide awake, in the stuffy little cabin. Harriet pushed herself up onto her elbow and explained what she was thinking.

'What can we do?' said Ben. 'Johnny Four Toes seems to be holding all the aces at the moment.' He paused. 'Where is this Point House you were talking about?'

'Angle Bay,' said Harriet. 'My father said it was an old haunt for pirates. He told me about someone called John Callice who used it, years and years ago. It seems as if Johnny and his men have done the same.'

They lapsed into silence. It would take Johnny a day

or so to resupply the *Caroline*. Perhaps a chance would come while the pirates were busy loading the yacht? Johnny had talked about sailing across the Atlantic. Perhaps he was intending to make for Hispaniola or Port Royal on Jamaica, some place in the Spanish Indies that he knew well. It would mean taking a lot of supplies on board and the pirates would be kept busy for hours. That looked to be their best chance.

They moored that night, Harriet guessed, off the coast of Pembrokeshire. None of the pirates would fancy the idea of tackling the rugged coastline with its treacherous currents and strong south-westerly winds in the dark and so they'd be happy to lie up and wait for daylight.

'That's fine,' said Harriet to Ben. 'The longer the delay in getting to the Point House the more chance there is of the Squire finding his way off the island.'

Ben nodded grimly but kept his thoughts to himself. Somebody brought them bread and water for their supper and they fell asleep to the sound of the wind whistling and howling through the rigging. Despite everything, Harriet slept soundly. Allowed up onto the deck the following morning, she was amazed to find that the storm had finally blown itself out during the night. It was a day of fresh breezes and fine sunshine. It was late on in the afternoon when the *Caroline* finally sighted the huge bulk of St Anne's Head over the starboard bow and, an hour later, they sailed into the broad expanse of Milford Haven. The yacht moved easily up the river, rounded the point and drew into East Angle Bay.

Standing on the quarter deck, Harriet watched the

pirates run out along the yard arms to quickly furl the sails and then stand waiting as the yacht began to lose way. Whatever else they might be, there was no denying that these men were excellent sailors, she thought. At Johnny's command, the bow cable was unleashed and, with a roar, the anchor dropped into the quiet waters of the bay. The *Caroline* had come to a serene halt.

'The Point House,' said Johnny Four Toes. A small white building, complete with straggling outhouses, lay nestled against the lower slopes of the headland, a bare hundred yards away. There was a short shingle foreshore in front of the building and Harriet could see figures moving around in one of the rooms. The front door of the house stood wide open.

'Look,' whispered Ben, 'I can even see the time on that clock.' He pointed towards the open door and Harriet followed the direction of his gaze. The boy was right. A large wooden-cased clock stood in the hallway of the Point House, both hands pointing towards the figure six at the bottom of its white face.

'Best anchorage in Wales,' said Johnny Four Toes, coming up silently and easily behind them. 'Even if your Squire does manage to get off the island, he'll never know we're here. For all he knows we could be two hundred miles away.'

He turned and, staring at one of his men, jerked his head in the direction of Harriet and Ben. 'Tom, best keep a weather eye on this pair.'

Harriet felt a heavy hand descend on her collar and she looked up into the hard, uncaring eyes of the pirate who had captured the *Caroline*.

It was the work of only a few minutes to batten down

the *Caroline*'s hatches and by half past seven they were heading across the bay to land on the shingle in front of the Point House. Harriet and Ben were herded up the bank and dragged into the hall of the inn.

'Stand there,' ordered Tom, pushing them back against the wall.

The hands on the clock, Harriet noticed, had still not moved – maybe someone should be reminded to wind the mechanism, she thought. Through the doorway into the bar, Harriet could see Johnny Four Toes standing in the centre of the room, talking urgently to a grey-haired old woman. Her face was lined and her complexion red from the wind.

'What do we have here?' the woman said, eyes fixing on Harriet and pointing through the open doorway. 'A bit young for your trade, eh, Johnny?'

Johnny looked up. 'They're nothing to concern you, Mrs Davies, just a little extra insurance.' His foot snaked out and kicked the door shut.

Harriet and Ben stood silently in the hallway as the pirates went about their business, constantly coming and going, in and out of the house. Tom did not move, his eyes fixed on the *Caroline* as she swung at her mooring a few hundred feet away.

Finally the bar door swung open and Johnny Four Toes came out into the hallway. Jeb followed closely behind. 'Our supplies will be here in the morning,' he smiled. 'A few hours to get them on board and by this time tomorrow we'll be away.'

Harriet stared at him. 'And us?' she asked, quietly.

Johnny glared at her but did not reply. Harriet felt her stomach grow huge – it was obvious what Johnny intended to do. With a snap of his fingers the pirate motioned Jeb forward. 'Lock them up!'

At pistol point they were pushed roughly up the stairs and thrust into a small, dark chamber. Two dirty mattresses lay on the floor but there was no other furniture and they were not offered a light.

'Sweet dreams,' sneered Jeb as he slammed shut the door behind them and locked it. 'Remember, I'll be waiting for you in the morning.'

They heard him laugh as his footsteps clattered down the wooden staircase. 'Twenty-four hours,' breathed Harriet. 'That's all we've got. The Squire will never be off the island by then. We've got to delay them.'

'Yes,' said Ben, 'but how?'

'There is only one way – the *Caroline*. Somehow or other we've got to stop them using the yacht.'

Ben nodded, knowing Harriet was right. But how could they do it? They were locked up in the Point House with the pirates down below and the *Caroline* lying off shore. She was close by but she might as well be moored on the moon.

'I know it's going to be difficult,' said Harriet at last, 'but we've got to do something to delay them. And the ship's the only way I can think of.'

'Do you mean sink her?'

Harriet shook her head. 'I wouldn't know how – would you? No, if we could just get on board, I think we could probably cut her cable. It'll be high water in a few hours and then the tide should start to ebb. Once that happens, we won't need to do anything, just wait for the elements. The tide should carry her ashore, on the other side of the bay with any luck. It won't sink her but it might take Johnny and his pirates a day or so to refloat her. And by that time the Squire and Mr Lort could just be here.'

Ben nodded uncertainly. When Johnny Four Toes discovered what they had done, his rage would be terrible. Harriet didn't like to think about what he might do to them. Ben seemed to sense her fear. Harriet glanced at the boy and shrugged with a nonchalance that neither of them really felt. 'Our lives are forfeit already, aren't they?' Harriet said. 'There's no way he's going to let us walk out of here. We might as well try to take him with us.'

She crossed to the window. The shutters were drawn and locked tight. By squinting through a small gap in the wood, she could see the silent shape of the *Caroline* in the evening sunshine. The yacht lay so close yet so far away, her reflection perfectly mirrored in the waters of the bay. And in the hold was the treasure that they had all worked so hard to find.

'Later tonight,' said Harriet, 'when it gets dark, we'll get out to the ship. For now we need to find a way of getting that shutter open.'

She stared around, searching for something to use as tool. Her eyes lighted on an empty bottle that stood in the fireplace. She strode across the room, picked up the bottle and held it out for Ben to see.

He looked at it doubtfully, then nodded. Harriet pulled a blanket off one of the mattresses and wrapped it around the bottle. Carefully, trying hard not to make too much noise, she rapped the package against the stone fireplace. There was a sharp crack as the bottle shattered. She paused and listened intently for the sound of footsteps on the stairs outside. There was nothing. The pirates were now too busy celebrating – the sound of singing and laughter from the bar below came wafting up through the floorboards.

Harriet took the largest piece of broken glass and began to gouge at the lock of the wooden shutter. The angle was awkward and the glass bit into her fingers. 'It's no good,' she cried, after a few minutes, 'I'm not having any effect.'

Ben ran his finger along the wood. 'You are, you know,' he said, 'but it's going to be a long, hard job. Better let me have a turn.' Between them, they spent the next hour working on the lock. The slightest mistake meant that the glass would slip and cut into their hands. Before long the floor beneath the window and even the casement itself were spotted with drops of blood.

Darkness fell, long shadows creeping gradually across the bay in front of them. Like fingers of doom, Harriet thought, trying hard to keep her imagination in check. From the room below the raucous bellowing of the drinkers rose and fell like the wind as the pirates celebrated their success late into the night. To Harriet, their victory meant that she and Ben and the Squire had failed and she tasted the bitterness of defeat in her throat. Like bile, it clung there, sweet and cloying.

The moon rose and set and still they worked on. It was well past midnight but even so, Harriet wasn't ready when Ben finally stood back from the window. He took a deep breath. 'I reckon that's enough. Let's try it now,' he said. He put his shoulder to the shutter and pushed. The wood groaned, then splintered and the casement flew open. In the room below the pirates sang on, oblivious.

'Ready?' said Harriet, climbing up onto the ledge.

Ben shook his head and put a restraining hand on her arm. 'I can move faster alone. And swimming, Harriet? How else can we get out to the yacht? You know you'd be more of a hindrance than a help.'

In her heart Harriet knew he was right. Just the thought of cold water closing in around her body made her squirm. She could run as fast as any of the boys in the village but she had always hated the water. So she nodded in agreement.

'I'll cut her loose and be back in an hour,' Ben said. 'Then, with any luck, we can get away before they discover the ship's gone.' He hoisted himself onto the ledge, and dropped out of view. Harriet walked to the window and listened. There was no sound from the beach below even though she knew that Ben would now be padding across the shingle. She smiled – his old poacher's instincts put to good use.

How long she stood at the casement Harriet never knew. The noise from the room below finally began to lessen and die as, one by one, the pirates fell asleep over their rum and beer. Harriet waited, fuming and worrying, but there was no sign of Ben.

'Come on,' she whispered, pacing nervously up and down the room. 'You should have been back an hour ago.'

She waited and waited until finally she could stand the inactivity no more. She would get out while she still could, she decided, and try to find out what had happened to Ben. He might be in serious trouble. She listened carefully and, hearing nothing, pulled herself up onto the window ledge.

At that moment there came the sound of a shoe scraping against the wall below and, heart racing, she dropped back into the room. 'Ben?'

There was no answer but within a few seconds she heard the sound of someone clambering up the ivy on the wall outside. She gathered herself, ready to pound any enemy who might be coming in through the open casement. It was with a surge of relief that she saw Ben's head appear over the windowsill. She uttered a silent prayer of gratitude, then grabbed hold of the boy's arm and pulled him inside.

'Did you do it?' she asked.

Ben lay gasping on the floor, clearly exhausted. Slowly he shook his head.

'But why? Why ever not?'

Ben was fighting hard to regain his breath. When he was at last able to speak, his reply was measured. 'Because,' he said, 'when I got there, the ship had vanished. Somebody had been there ahead of me, Harriet. The anchorage is empty – the *Caroline* has gone!'

*Chapter Nine*

# Mutiny

Harriet sat back on one of the mattresses, her face clouded by amazement and disbelief. She stared up at Ben. 'Who could have taken her?'

Ben shook his head and smoothed back his soaking hair. He picked up a blanket and began to dry himself. 'It was pitch dark when I got to the water's edge and I had to feel my way over the mud. I swam out to where I reckoned the yacht was lying but when I reached the spot, there was nothing there. No yacht, no longboat, nothing. At first I thought I'd got my directions wrong and so I swam around, trying to find her. Still no sign. And then the moon came out and I could take a breather and look around. She wasn't there, Harriet, not anywhere in the bay. Somebody has moved the ship.'

Harriet scratched her head, her mind working furiously. Who on earth would have moved the *Caroline* at this time of night? And – more importantly – why?

'Johnny Four Toes?' she said. 'Could he have done it?'

'I shouldn't think so,' Ben said. 'He'd have no cause to do that. And besides, I could hear him singing down-stairs as I went across the shingle. I can't see why any of the pirates would want to move her – as Johnny said, this is an excellent anchorage. And they need her as close to the Point House as possible so they can get their stores on board in the morning.'

He paused and glanced meaningfully at Harriet. 'No, I reckon there's something else. I don't know who he is but I think someone else is trying to delay Johnny Four Toes too – somebody apart from us.'

Harriet pursed her lips and thought about her concerns of the past few weeks. Somebody had been watching, of that she was sure. Even Johnny had said as much. A cold shiver ran swiftly up her back. 'I think we should get away while we can,' she said.

Dawn had begun to break, long rosy-red fingers of light streaking across the eastern sky. Already Harriet could pick out the hill on the other side of the bay. They had to move now, she thought, before it grew too light. She didn't like the idea of being pursued across the headland by the drunken cut-throats from the room below. 'Let's go,' she said.

They moved to the casement window and at that moment the door to the bedroom crashed open, hammering back against the wall with a boom as loud as thunder. Harriet's heart jumped in fright as she spun towards the sound. Johnny Four Toes stood in the doorway, his body filling the frame. Outlined against the light from the corridor outside, he seemed huge and powerful and dangerous. 'Been swimming, boy?' he said.

Harriet leapt for him, fingers clawing and desperation in her eyes. But the pirate was too quick and sidestepped her charge. As Harriet flailed past him, Johnny smashed downwards with his fist. The blow took her on the top of her skull and Harriet felt the edges of the world grow misty and grey. She had a sudden glimpse of Ben's horror-stricken face, then she fell forward onto her hands and knees on the floor. As if from very far away she heard voices echoing through the grey mist.

'You've killed her,' Ben was shouting.

Johnny shook his head. 'Not yet, boy, I need her alive. And I need to know what you've done with my ship.' He turned and spoke urgently to someone outside the door. Two pirates pushed their way into the room and dragged Harriet to her feet.

'Downstairs!' Johnny ordered.

A blast of cold air from the open front door helped Harriet regain her senses. For the briefest of moments they paused before the door, gazing out at the empty anchorage and Harriet's world stopped spinning. Johnny Four Toes swore under his breath and Harriet and Ben were dragged into the bar. Her head ached but she saw clearly that the room was filled with pirates, many the worse for drink, holding their heads with unsteady hands. Harriet and Ben were pushed into a seat before the window. Johnny stood above them, breathing heavily, and visibly trying to control his fury. 'Well?' he demanded. 'Where's the yacht?'

Harriet sat back in the chair, feeling with her fingers at the lump on the back of her head. Despite her fear, despite the pain, she somehow managed to smile at Ben. He grinned back at her.

'I wish we knew,' he said. 'But even if we did, we wouldn't tell you.'

'Damn you, boy . . .' Johnny Four Toes reached out to grab him, murder in his eyes.

Despite the sickness churning in her belly, Harriet leapt to her feet. Clutching at Johnny's hands, she managed to push her way in front of him. She glared at

Johnny, shielding the boy with her slender body. 'He doesn't know, he really doesn't. Honest.'

She stared around, desperately trying to find the words that would keep these men from killing them there and then. 'All right, we did plan to take the yacht. We cut open the shutter and Ben climbed out. He swam to the yacht but when he reached her, she wasn't there. Somebody else had already moved her.'

For a few moments there was silence as Johnny Four Toes digested the information. Finally he nodded. Weak with relief, Harriet slumped down alongside Ben.

'Hellfire and damnation!' shouted Jeb, suddenly, from his seat at the bar. 'Are you going to believe this rubbish, Johnny? They must know who has taken the ship. And the treasure, too. If they won't tell you where they've put her, I say we beat it out of them – now!' He leapt to his feet and advanced across the room, cutlass half drawn and a cold snarl upon his face. Johnny Four Toes watched him coming, then swung easily around to face him. Smiling, he placed his hand on the big man's chest and let it rest there.

'Jeb, Jeb,' he said, 'think about it carefully. This ain't the time to let your temper get the better of you. What the girl says is probably true. Ask yourself this question – if they knew who'd taken the ship, would they still be here? Here in the Point House along with us? Well, would they? Of course not, they'd be long gone. The boy is still wet from his dip in the sea so it's my bet that what the girl says is right.'

Jeb stared at him, uncertain and suddenly afraid. He could see Black Bart's treasure disappearing from under his eyes. Johnny Four Toes pushed home his advantage.

'Whoever took the ship can't have got far. There's two sailing boats as belongs to the Point House – we can have them rigged and sailing in a few minutes. If the ship's out there, we'll have her in our hands again before sunset.'

A low grumble of assent came from the pirates. Jeb shrugged and cast one last, long look in the direction of Harriet and Ben. 'Fair enough, Johnny, but I warn you, if we don't find that ship and our treasure, somebody is going to pay – and I don't rightly care who it is!' The challenge in his voice was unmistakable.

Johnny Four Toes smiled easily at him and spread his hands, placating. 'We'll find her, Jeb. Trust me.'

Jeb glared at him. 'Trust you? I'd as soon trust a bilge rat. You'd just better be right, Johnny.'

He turned and walked away. Johnny swung around to Harriet and Ben and spoke low and urgently out of the side of his mouth. 'If you value your lives, say and do nothing, unless I tell you.'

Within minutes the Point House became a scene of frantic activity. The inn's two sailing boats, launched and crewed by half a dozen pirates apiece, set off across the bay. Another group ran off along the headland, cutlasses and pistols in hand, while a final group set off to scour the foreshore to the south.

Soon only Johnny Four Toes was left, standing at the inn doorway, deep in thought and watching their progress. His wiry figure seemed to sag in the door-frame. 'Things are beginning to turn a little difficult for me, my young friends,' he said at last. 'I must confess, losing the ship and the treasure is something I hadn't reckoned with. That's fair done me.'

Smiling ruefully, he threw himself down in the chair opposite Harriet. 'You've been a thorn in my side, girl, right from the beginning of this affair. And if things go against me, I reckon as how it'll be down to you, more than anyone else. You've shown courage and that's something I admire. But I'll tell you one thing, both of you, your lives have never been in more danger than they are at this moment. Once old Jeb gets his temper up, there's no saying where things will finish.'

'We don't know anything about the yacht,' Harriet said, pleading. 'Where she's gone or who's taken her.'

Johnny stilled her with a raised hand. 'It doesn't matter. If Jeb thinks you were involved, then your lives hang by a thread. If we can't find that gold today, I reckon it'll be a case of them deposing me. That's how it is with gentlemen of fortune, a true democracy if ever there was one. If they think I've failed them, they'll get rid of me quick as that!'

He snapped his fingers, the sound echoing around the silent room. 'They'll vote in a new captain. And if Jeb takes command, nobody will be able to hold him.'

'Why not let us go, then?' said Ben. 'Now, before they come back.'

Johnny raised his eyebrows. 'And what do you think will happen to me when they come back and find you gone? No, not yet, my friend. Like I told you before, this cruise has still got a long way to run. If we can find that ship in the next few hours, we can still get away with the gold. The game's not up yet, not by a long shot.'

He paused. 'But if we don't find the ship, then I'm going to need some extra insurance – and that comes in the shape of you two! You're more valuable to me now than ever before. I'll keep you alive, at least I'll try my best. If things go wrong, saving you two might just be enough to keep me from the rope. Remember I tried to help you, eh? Remember that and put in a good word for old Johnny Four Toes if it's needed.'

His face was suddenly sly and Harriet knew there was nothing this man would not do in order to save his own skin.

Morning turned to afternoon and still no news came of the *Caroline*. Whoever had spirited her away had done a first class job. It seemed as if the yacht – and the treasure in her hold – had disappeared from the face of the earth.

As the pirates trooped disconsolately back to the Point House, there was an angry mood of rebellion in the air. Nobody looked at Johnny Four Toes but kept their eyes fixed firmly on the floor or on the back of the man in front. Nobody spoke but the silence was more eloquent than a million words. The mood of the men was dangerous and it was clear where most of them were putting the blame for the loss of the treasure.

Harriet and Ben sat quietly in the bar alongside Johnny. Each time the inn door opened, Harriet jumped, every nerve jangling. She dreaded seeing Jeb. She knew he'd put the blame on them and she feared his temper. She wished to heaven that the *Caroline* were still anchored in the bay. Who could have taken her? It had been bad enough being at the mercy of Johnny Four Toes, but Jeb was far, far worse. Their lives would not be worth much, hers or Ben's, if the *Caroline* wasn't found.

At last there was a crunch on the shingle outside. The

room fell silent as everyone – pirates and captives alike – waited for Jeb. He came slamming in through the door, his jacket stained with mud and his hair wild and dishevelled. Cursing, he forced his way to the bar, scattering the pirates before him.

'Nothing!' he snarled to the waiting room. 'Not a glimpse of the damned ship. She's sunk without trace.' He grabbed a bottle of rum and took a long pull before slamming it down onto the bar and turning to face his crew mates. Nobody dared to speak as his eyes swept around the group. His gaze finally fell on Johnny Four Toes. 'Unless somebody knows something the rest of us don't? What do you say, Johnny, was this all part of your plan? Is there something you want to tell us, some trick you haven't told us about?'

Johnny was all affability. 'What do you mean by that, Jeb? There's no trick, no plan, apart from the one we hatched between us all those months ago.'

Jeb sneered and turned back for the rum bottle. 'Maybe – and then again, maybe not. But whichever way you look at it, I still reckons as you've fouled up this 'ere cruise. We had Black Bart's gold, every last farthing of it. We didn't need to come back here. That was your idea – and a damned stupid one it was, too. Well, now we've lost the treasure – and in a case like that it's always the captain as takes the blame. I told you it was bad luck to bring those damned kids along. I reckon as they've been a jinx on this 'ere cruise.'

Johnny smiled at him, that dangerous and deadly smile Harriet knew so well. Slowly he levered himself to his feet and stood facing Jeb. 'Fancy a turn as captain, do you, Jeb, fancy being in control of things for a little while? You always did have big ideas, Jeb Turner, ideas above your station. Perhaps you think you can do better than old Johnny Four Toes?'

'Perhaps,' said Jeb. 'I reckons as I couldn't do much worse, that's for certain.'

Johnny sniffed disdainfully and shook his head. 'You haven't got the brains of a mongrel dog, Jeb. If you'd been in charge, we wouldn't have got half as far. And now you want to throw old Johnny over?'

Jeb did not reply but he held his gaze firm and stared Johnny straight in the eye. For five seconds there was silence in the room.

'You know what to do, Jeb,' said Johnny, at last. 'If you're unhappy with the way I've run things on this cruise, there's a process to follow. You know our way – if you think you're man enough.'

He turned on his heel, contemptuously dismissing Jeb. Then he glanced back and spat, deliberately and accurately, over his shoulder. The spittle hit Jeb's boot and lay there like an accusation. The big pirate's face turned crimson with rage and the veins stood out like string on his neck. With a roar of anger, he snatched up his cutlass and charged. Johnny spun around and, before anyone could blink, ducked under the man's sword arm. His head shot up and caught Jeb underneath the chin, the force of the blow smashing the pirate backwards. Then Johnny leapt forward and buried his knife up to the hilt in Jeb's belly. The big sailor coughed, his feet slipping and sliding on the floor, and clutched weakly at the hilt of the knife. His eyes stared in surprise.

'Too slow, my friend,' said Johnny, twisting the knife and giving the wounded sailor a shove that sent him sprawling onto the floor. 'You always were so easy to rile, Jeb, never could keep your temper.'

Harriet watched in horror as he bent over the body, put his foot on Jeb's chest and pulled out his knife. Then, carefully and coldly, he stabbed again, once to the throat. Jeb's feet twitched and finally fell still.

'Anyone else?' Johnny asked as he straightened up. 'Anyone else fancy taking command?' He glared at the pirates, defying any of them to speak or move. 'You, Tom? You maybe fancy the job?'

Tom backed away, hands raised. 'No, Johnny. No.'

Johnny stared at the assembled group. Everyone seemed to be cowering back, amazed at the ease with which Johnny Four Toes had dealt with Jeb. Johnny was not the man to pass up his opportunity. 'Damn all your hides for a bunch of cowardly lubbers,' he growled. 'This girl has got more courage than the whole lot of you lumped together.'

He half turned towards Harriet, then back to face the pirates once more. 'All right, we may have lost the treasure but we've still got our skins. Remember that. The most important thing is to get away from this place. Now, I'm still in command here and I need some time to think. So give a man some space so as he can plan what we're going to do next. In the meantime, Tom, get that dog of a mutineer out of here.'

He gestured towards Jeb's body and picked up the half-empty bottle of rum from the bar. Then he went carefully across to Harriet and Ben and sat in the chair alongside them. He drank deeply and luxuriously from the bottle, smiled at Harriet and winked.

*Chapter Ten*

# The Final Battle

'Well,' said Ben, leaning close and whispering into Harriet's ear, 'what do you think about your new best friend? Do you really think he means what he says about keeping us in one piece?'

Harriet kept her voice low. 'I wouldn't trust him as far as I could throw him. Remember, he's the one who killed old Jethro. And you saw how he dealt with Jeb. He's a ruthless killer. He'll do anything to save himself.'

It was late on in the evening and the pirates lay slumped around the Point House, some of them staring wistfully into space, others already fast asleep. The supply of rum and other alcohol had dried up. With the treasure gone and with no immediate possibility of getting it back, it seemed as if Mrs Davies, the landlady, had decided the pirates were a bad credit risk.

All day Johnny Four Toes had been like a caged tiger, prowling around the inn, his face clouded by a scowl as black as midnight. Nobody spoke to him and he spoke to nobody. Every so often, however, he would glance quietly across to Harriet and smile. It made her shiver.

At evening foul-smelling oil lamps were brought into the bar and shadows suddenly leapt like dancers at a May Fair across the ceilings and walls. Harriet's mind was racing. So much had happened over the past few weeks; so many men had died in the search for wealth and fortune. Black Bart's gold? They could keep it, Harriet decided, wishing with all her heart that she had never bought the map off old Jethro. If I had not been so fascinated by the story of the pirates and their gold, she asked herself, would Jethro and the yacht captain, Thomson and so many others, still be alive? At last her head dropped forward onto her chest and she slept.

She was awoken by the sound of Johnny Four Toes's voice. His energy restored, he was standing in the centre of the room, shouting at the sleeping pirates. 'Come on, you lubbers, it's almost morning. Time to go! Outside everyone, outside now!'

Harriet and Ben pushed themselves to their feet and followed the sailors as they trooped, yawning and unhappy, through the front door of the Point House. 'What's got into him this morning?' whispered Ben.

Harriet shrugged. 'Perhaps he's come up with a plan, some idea to get them all away from here before anyone finds out what they've done.'

Unwillingly, they formed up in a shallow semi-circle in front of the inn. The sun was beginning to rise over the hills at the eastern end of the bay but there was little warmth in the day. Harriet shivered and tried to bury her chin in the soft collar of her coat.

'Right, my hearties,' Johnny declared, face beaming and voice alive with hope, 'this is what we are going to do. Pembroke town lies just over there.' He pointed across the bay. 'Ten miles at most, just a gentle stroll before breakfast for men like us. Pembroke is the largest port in west Wales – over 200 ships are registered there, all working out of the quay below the castle. We're going to walk into town and choose ourselves one of those ships. Then we're off on the account again.'

He paused to let the effect of his words sink in.

For a minute, perhaps, there was silence but soon the grumbling started. 'What's he saying? I don't want to go to sea again.'

'How are we going to get a ship?'

'What about Black Bart's gold?'

Johnny glared at the speakers. 'Listen, lads, we've played our hand in this business and we've lost. The gold has gone, that's all there is to it. We'll go to Pembroke and find ourselves another boat, an easy target. Most of the crews will be ashore in the ale houses and we can take our pick and be away before anybody even knows we're there. Then we can live the only life gentlemen of fortune like us should ever want to live – on the account.'

Harriet watched the pirates carefully. Most of them were now nodding their heads in agreement. What Johnny said made sense and they knew it.

'He's right,' said one of them. 'Piracy's all we know.'

'Off on the account,' breathed another. 'That's the life for us.'

Johnny Four Toes swung suddenly round to face Tom. 'And what do you say, young Tom?'

Tom must be the last real threat to Johnny's power, Harriet thought. Once he gives in, there's no-one to threaten him and he'll turn on us again.

Tom was no hero and just shrugged, clearly remembering how Johnny had dealt with Jeb.

'Suits me,' he said. 'Let's get started.'

'Aye, lad,' Johnny whispered, almost to himself. 'Soonest there, soonest we'll be away I reckon.'

Harriet shuddered. Would she and Ben be forced to go on the account too? Or would Johnny see no further need for 'insurance' once the pirate crew was on the high seas? At any rate he needed them now. Tom was under strict orders to keep them close. 'Don't even think about escaping?' he growled at the two prisoners, pushing them roughly into the heart of the pirate crew, and running his finger menacingly along his cutlass.

Harriet watched as he turned his face to the road that led around the headland and towards the village of Angle. At that moment a musket fired from close at hand, the roar of the explosion reverberating through the still morning air. Tom gasped in surprise, clutched at his chest and fell forward onto the shingle. His foot kicked once and then he lay still. Almost before he had hit the ground, there was the sound of shouting.

'Surrender, damn you!' The tone was familiar and with a sudden lift of her heart, Harriet recognised Squire Campbell's voice. Before Johnny or any of the pirates could move, half a dozen red-coated soldiers trotted around the corner of the house behind them. Their muskets were raised and pointed, not just at the sailors, but at Ben and Harriet, trapped in their midst. Harriet looked from one crew to the other, her heart a crazy drumbeat, her limbs crawling with fear. Muskets or cutlasses, it made no difference.

A second group of soldiers suddenly ghosted over the sea wall, muskets poised and bayonets glinting in the morning sunlight. Then the Squire and Mr Lort were astride the path, blocking the way into the village. Alongside them stood a small, dark man Harriet didn't recognise.

For five seconds everyone froze. Then, the spell was broken. 'Run!' screamed one of the pirates and the next moment there was complete pandemonium.

Frightened pirates darted like snipe across the foreshore and the headland, but all the escape routes had been blocked. One or two tried to make a fight of it but their cutlasses and knives were no use against the muskets and bayonets of the soldiers.

Shocked by the smell of powder, the flash of fire and the shouts of the fleeing men, Harriet couldn't move, her legs still glued to the spot. 'All rounded up, Squire,' she heard the officer in charge of the soldiers announce. 'Two dead, three wounded, the rest all prisoners.'

Suddenly she was aware of Ben, standing beside her, and a young officer, still hot from the fray, pushing them towards the Squire. She half fell, half ran in her relief at seeing her old friend once again. The Squire was beaming from ear to ear. Then he glanced at Harriet and winked. The gesture seemed to free her at last.

'How?' asked Harriet, bounding up to him and grabbing at his arm. 'However did you get here?'

The Squire grinned and hugged her tightly. 'All in good time, Harriet, all in good time.' He turned towards the officer. 'Their leader? You've got him?'

'Yes, sir.'

The Squire led the way back to the Point House. Johnny Four Toes was standing in the open doorway, a soldier's long bayonet levelled steadily at his throat. When he saw the Squire, he spread his arms in a helpless, resigned gesture. It was a forced movement that did not even begin to hide his bitterness.

'Well played, Squire,' he said. 'You've caught me this time, good and fair.'

Squire Campbell nodded solemnly. 'Not without a little help, I must confess.'

He turned and gestured to the man standing behind him. It was the small, dark man from the roadway. Suddenly Harriet knew who it must be. 'Allow me,' said the Squire, 'to present Joseph Stephenson, late of Black Bart's ship *Royal Fortune*.'

He turned again to Johnny Four Toes. 'But then, of course, you already know each other.'

Johnny was dumbstruck. His mouth opened but no sound came out. A sudden sweat had broken out across his forehead and lay there like tiny drops of rain. Stephenson stared into Johnny's eyes and then bowed, mockingly. His voice, when he spoke, was low and raw, as if his throat had been recently raked with grapeshot.

'Mr Jessup, you cannot know how good it is to see you again. It's been a long time – too long, I suspect.'

Johnny gulped. A spasm of fear shot across his face but then he seemed to pull himself together. 'But I thought you were dead,' he gasped, 'killed on the *Fortune* along with Bart.'

'As you can see,' said Nicholas Lort, 'he clearly wasn't. You, on the other hand, soon will be – swinging on a rope at Execution Dock.'

'I think, perhaps, we should continue this conversation inside,' said the Squire, leading the way into the inn.

They sat around the table in the wide window seat and the Squire called for Mrs Davies. She came hurriedly, wringing her hands and not sure where to look.

'Whatever you want, Squire,' she said, 'whatever your pleasure, all on the house, sir, all at my expense. Always a pleasure to serve you, Squire Campbell.'

She stole a furtive glance at Johnny Four Toes. 'These pirates descended on me only the other day, Squire. They took over my house and kept those poor children prisoner upstairs in my own chamber. I was so afraid, frightened out of my wits. You know me, sir, I'm only a poor widow woman trying to make a living. I hope you'll not be thinking me one of them?'

Squire Campbell glared at her and the woman quailed before his gaze. 'Your part in this affair will not be forgotten. It will be investigated and we will have to see what becomes of you. For now, I want wine – the best in the house, mind. Only the best will do.'

The Squire poured the ruby liquid into their glasses while Mrs Davies quickly disappeared from view. Johnny Four Toes sat staring at Joseph Stephenson. He could not take his eyes off the man and Harriet was reminded of what Lort had told her on the *Caroline*, how Stephenson had sworn revenge on Johnny Four Toes.

'Tell us how you came here, sir,' said Harriet at last. 'How did you get off the island? How on earth did you manage to find us?'

The Squire leaned back in his chair and pointed to Joseph Stephenson. 'For that we have to thank our friend here. Perhaps he should tell you.'

Stephenson, too, had eyes only for his old shipmate. He had fixed Johnny with an iron stare as soon as they sat down and his eyes never left the pirate's face, even when he began to speak. 'I've been watching you for weeks,' he said grimly, 'all of you – you, girl, you, boy, even the Squire. But most of all I've been watching my old friend here.'

The watcher in the woods, Harriet thought. This was the man who had been dogging their tracks, following them all, keeping everyone under surveillance.

'I knew you would lead Johnny to Bart's treasure, sooner or later. As soon as the girl got the map off Jethro, I knew where it would end. Now, I had a pretty good tail on my friend Johnny Four Toes and, more importantly, he didn't know I was there.'

Johnny snorted. 'Oh, I knew you were there, all right. Leastways, I knew somebody was watching. I'm damned if I thought it was you, though.'

Stephenson nodded and grinned. 'That's what I hoped you'd feel. I could have finished you at any time, Johnny, but that wasn't what I wanted. I wanted you to get your hands on that treasure – and then I wanted you to lose it. I wanted you to feel the pain of that, right enough.' He broke off and glanced, quickly, at Harriet and Ben. His gaze soon flickered back to the stricken face of Johnny Four Toes but when he spoke again it was to the whole group.

'I followed Johnny and his men, just like they were following you, all the way up the coast. It wasn't an easy task, I can tell you, sailing single handed and trying to keep myself hidden at the same time. When he left the Squire and Mr Lort on the island, I just waited until he was over the horizon and then came ashore.'

Lort carefully folded his arms across his chest and glared at Johnny. 'Less than two hours, my friend, that's all it took. Less than two hours and we were off the island.'

Stephenson leaned across the table and coldly, deliberately, poured wine into Johnny's glass. The pirate sneered and pushed it away.

'It was something of a crush,' said Stephenson, 'getting everyone into my little sailing boat, but we were behind you all the way. We even watched you scuttle the lugger. After that it was just a matter of finding ourselves a bigger vessel and biding our time.'

'You knew he'd come here,' said Harriet, 'to the Point House?'

Stephenson nodded. 'It stood to reason. This has always been a good hideaway for gentlemen of fortune. He'd used the place many times before, just like me.'

'And you took the *Caroline*,' Harriet said, understanding dawning on her. 'You cut her loose?'

Squire Campbell nodded. 'That he did, Harriet. Late at night, while the pirates were celebrating, we rowed into the bay and Stephenson cut her cable and sailed her away. She's safe and sound in Stackpole Quay. The treasure is being unloaded and taken to Stackpole Court, even as we speak. Your father – and yours, Ben – have been most helpful in that respect.'

'The soldiers?'

'They're from Pembroke. I thought we might need a little help to deal with our friend and his murderous crew and so I spoke to the garrison commander.'

Harriet's mind was working furiously. There was still so much she needed to know. She turned to face Stephenson. 'You escaped after the final battle, Black Bart's final battle, off Parrot Island?' she asked.

'Aye, girl,' Stephenson nodded. 'After Bart was killed, I managed to slip away. It was easy enough in the confusion. I escaped, went to ground and spent the next twenty years hunting that man.' He pointed to Johnny Four Toes, his lip curling into a snarl. 'He betrayed Bart Roberts, hoping to get his hands on the money. Twenty years it's taken me, twenty years of slipping and sliding around the world, but I wouldn't have changed one moment of it.'

By now Johnny Four Toes had regained his self control. He glared at Stephenson, his cold dark eyes filled with murder and hate. 'Damn you, Jos Stephenson,' he cursed. 'Between you and that girl you've fair brought me down.'

Stephenson drained his glass and sat back in his chair. 'I swore I'd avenge Bart Roberts. He wasn't just a pirate; he was the greatest pirate of us all. But more than that, he was a friend, a true friend. And that morning on the *Royal Fortune*, when he died because of your greed and treachery, I knew that I had only one aim left in life – to find you and bring you down.'

The air went suddenly cold. 'I reckon as how I've done that, Johnny Four Toes,' Stephenson smiled, taking his eyes from the pirate's face for almost the first time, 'and now I can die happy.'

'That's exactly what you'll do,' yelled Johnny. Before anyone could move, he lunged forward. A knife had suddenly appeared in his hand. His arm cut a wide arc through the air and struck once at Stephenson's chest. The small man made barely a sound but slumped back in his chair.

'That's for you, Jos Stephenson,' hissed Johnny. He smiled, briefly, at Harriet, inclining his head in a gesture that was slow and almost elegant, then turned and leapt for the window. To Harriet it was as if the events of the next few moments were taking place in slow motion. She knew Johnny was trying to escape but she could not have moved if she had been paid a thousand guineas.

'Hold him!' cried Lort.

The window shattered in an explosion of glass and wood. At the same moment Lort and the soldier fired their pistols, the gunshots echoing around the room with ear-splitting force.

'No!' screamed Harriet as everyone dived towards the window. 'Don't let him escape!'

Summoning all her strength, she levered herself to her feet and followed the Squire and Lort to peer through the shattered casement. Johnny Four Toes was lying motionless on the shingle outside. His limbs had become strangely shapeless, like those of a discarded rag doll. The pistol shots had found their mark. Johnny Four Toes was dead.

Despite everything, despite all the horror that the man had unleashed, Harriet felt a momentary pang of pity. Seeing him lying there amongst the debris from the broken casement, she suddenly realised how vulnerable he looked. And then she shook her head as she remembered all he had done. Johnny Four Toes was the most evil man she had ever met. She remembered old Jethro lying in the hedge with his throat cut, the dead body of Jeb in this very room, and her pity disappeared.

Squire Campbell gently put his arm around Harriet's shoulder and pulled her away from the window. 'Perhaps it is better this way,' he said. 'It will save the cost of a trial. And it strikes me he would have wanted it to end like this.'

'Squire?' Behind them, Ben was leaning over the small, silent shape of Joseph Stephenson. The man had not moved since Johnny's attack and now the Squire strode urgently to his side. Stephenson was alive but only just.

'I'll get help,' said Lort, moving to the door.

Stephenson shook his head, weakly.

'Too late. I might have done for Johnny but he's finished me, too.' His hand fluttered across his chest and came away tinged with blood. 'One favour, Squire,' he whispered.

Squire Campbell leaned close, trying hard to catch the final words of the dying man. 'Anything.'

Stephenson coughed and a thin stream of blood began to inch down his chin. 'Build a memorial for Bart Roberts, so people will remember his name. It doesn't matter about me but he was the greatest . . .'

His voice trailed off and there was silence in the room. Squire Campbell reached down and gently closed the eyes of the dead man. 'He may have been a pirate,' he said, 'just like those men outside, but he saved our lives. And for that I'll never forget him. I'll build a memorial for his pirate chief.'

For several moments nobody spoke. Then, at last, the Squire put up his hands, straightened his coat collar and turned to Harriet and Ben. He smiled at them. 'I think that in the last week or so you young people have seen enough death and bloodshed to last a thousand years. But now it's all over. Let's get back to Stackpole. There are people waiting for us there and we all have a great deal of money to count.'

Despite everything that had happened over the past

few hours, Harriet began to smile. What the Squire had said was true. Her great adventure was finished and her parents would be waiting for her in their cottage in the village. She needed the familiarity of that tiny house alongside the village green, at least for the moment. Soon everything would be changing. She knew, before too long, that she would be leaving the cottage. She was rich, richer than she had ever thought possible, and from this point onwards nothing could ever be the same.

'It's been exciting though, hasn't it?' said Ben, guessing her thoughts and grinning at her.

They stood in the bar as the Squire strode out through the door into the sunshine. Ben nudged Harriet with his elbow. 'Perhaps now you can settle down to a peaceful life in the country?'

She stared at him and, together, they began to laugh. A quiet life would never be enough for Harriet – and Ben knew it. She reached down onto the table and picked up her half-empty glass of wine. 'Here's to the next time,' she said, carefully, 'wherever and whatever it might be!'